A bullet ricocheted off the front fender with a metallic thud.

"Stay down," Shane whispered harshly.

"Don't worry. I'm too scared to move." Kara's breath came in quick, shallow gasps. "We're trapped here."

"I'm taking care of this guy. We're sitting ducks."

"No." She clutched his arm. "You can't go out there. You don't know where he is. You could walk right into a bullet."

"I'm not letting him get to you."

"It's too dangerous."

"Then we'll freeze to death." Shane slipped his gun from his holster. "We can't just sit here."

"If he kills you, we're both dead," she whispered.

Shane reached for his radio and called dispatch. Nothing but static met his plea.

Kara's heart was pounding hard enough to make her chest burn.

Shane was right about one thing. Waiting for the killer to come to them was

D0205624

Sherri Shackelford is an award-winning author of inspirational books featuring ordinary people discovering extraordinary love. A reformed pessimist, Sherri has a passion for storytelling. Her books are fast paced and heartfelt with a generous dose of humor. She loves to hear from readers at sherri@sherrishackelford.com. Visit her website at sherrishackelford.com.

Books by Sherri Shackelford

Love Inspired Suspense

No Safe Place
Killer Amnesia
Stolen Secrets
Arctic Christmas Ambush

Visit the Author Profile page at Harlequin.com.

ARCTIC
CHRISTMAS
AMBUSH

SHERRI
SHACKELFORD

LOVE INSPIRED SUSPENSE
INSPIRATIONAL ROMANCE

LOVE INSPIRED® SUSPENSE
INSPIRATIONAL ROMANCE

ISBN-13: 978-1-335-40325-4

Arctic Christmas Ambush

Recycling programs for this product may not exist in your area.

This edition published by arrangement with Harlequin Books S.A.

For questions and comments about the quality of this book, please contact us at CustomerService@Harlequin.com.

Love Inspired
22 Adelaide St. West, 40th Floor
Toronto, Ontario M5H 4E3, Canada
www.Harlequin.com

Printed in U.S.A.

And not only so, but we glory in tribulations also:
knowing that tribulation worketh patience;
And patience, experience; and experience, hope.
–Romans 5:3-4

Dedicated to:

The law firm of Nielsen Miller-McCoy for their assistance in researching the wild and wacky world of real estate law. The truth, as they say, is often stranger than fiction.

ONE

The gunman was still in the house.

Kara Riley sank deeper into the jumble of suffocating winter coats in the hall closet. A metal zipper scraped her cheek, and the stale scent of mothballs turned her stomach.

She had to stay calm and think if she was going to survive the next few minutes.

Noises sounded from the kitchen, and her hands trembled.

Breathe, Kara, she silently coached herself. If she didn't get some oxygen into her lungs, she was going to faint.

An hour earlier, she'd parked her snow machine outside Walt's kennels in order to check on his litter of five-week-old pups. The falling snow was rapidly turning to blizzard conditions, and she was the only veterinarian within fifty miles.

She and Walt had known each other for more than a dozen years, and he always kept a carafe of coffee warming on the stove when he knew she was coming. Once she'd finished examining the animals, she'd let herself inside through the kitchen at the back of the house, as was her usual custom.

She was wiping her boots on the mat when she realized Walt was arguing with another man. Their voices were muffled through the wool flaps covering her ears, but there was no disguising the tone. She'd taken an automatic step deeper into the house before she heard the gunshot.

Walt's voice went abruptly silent and then there was a sickening thud.

She'd frozen in shock until the footfalls sounded. Acting on pure adrenaline and instinct, she'd ducked into the nearest hiding place—the closet beside the back door.

Trembling in silence, she listened as the gunman rummaged through the kitchen. Silverware rattled. A cupboard door slammed. Had he seen her snow machine parked behind the kennels? He couldn't have. Not from the house, anyway.

Please, God, please don't let him look inside the closet.

She hadn't been able to pull the door shut entirely, and a shaft of light appeared through the opening. Footfalls sounded, and a shadow passed before her hiding place. Panic flooded her system.

Backed against the wall, she twitched the sleeve of Walt's parka to fill the gap between the coats. If the gunman opened the door, he might not see her immediately. *Might not.* Her heart thudded against her ribs.

She held her breath until the footsteps receded.

Moving carefully, she reached for her phone to turn off the sound. The waterproof material of her parka rustled, and she cringed. Shielding the illuminated screen of her phone with one hand, she muted the sound. There was no way she was dying because of a text message alert.

The name at the top of her Favorite Contacts list snagged her attention: Shane Taylor.

Having dated the most senior Alaska state trooper assigned to the area was an advantage. She had his personal number. Even given the way things had ended between them, she knew he'd always be there for her. They were wrong for each other, that was all.

Kara typed her message and hit Send, then added another silent prayer.

How long before he responded? Shane wasn't always great about checking his personal messages, and given the current weather conditions, he was most likely distracted.

The footfalls neared, and a shiver of horror tripped down her spine. The puffy, down-filled parka blocked most of her vision. Walt's killer could be staring at the closet. There was no way to tell.

A doorknob rattled.

Pressing her hands against her mouth, she stifled a gasp.

For a long moment, the only sound was the blood rushing in her ears.

Then the back door slammed, but her relief was cut short when she heard the killer walk back into the kitchen.

Her shoulders sagged as he passed the closet and his heavy footsteps moved off. The front door opened and closed. But she didn't dare move. Not yet. Not until she knew for certain the killer wasn't coming back.

Sudden tears flooded her eyes. What if Walt was alive and she was cowering in the closet? *No.* She mentally shook her head. She couldn't think like that. If she left her hiding place too soon, they'd both be dead.

Seconds passed. No noises sounded. No doors opened.

No footsteps made their way down the hall. She gathered her courage and cautiously emerged from her shelter.

The house was eerily still. Wind whistled through the eaves, covering the sound of her raspy breathing.

She moved cautiously, her boots leaving watery footprints over the chipped tile. Walt had retired to his family home in Kodiak Springs, Alaska, the year before. The house was little more than a ramshackle cabin on a beautiful plot of land overlooking the hot springs resort, and no one had lived there since Walt's mom passed away five years before. He'd been slowly making repairs, but the place was barely habitable. Typical of Walt, he'd started on the kennels first.

As she rounded the corner to the living room, the smell hit her like a wall. *Blood.* Pungent and sickly sweet. A scent you only had to experience once to remember forever.

She stood paralyzed, knowing her life was about to change forever and unable to accept the truth.

A stack of firewood flanked the grate to her left. The Christmas tree in the corner was lit. A threadbare rag rug rested beneath her feet. Steeling herself against what she'd find, she lifted her gaze.

A sob caught in the back of her throat. She'd seen enough death in her life and veterinary training to know that Walt was gone.

Grief sapped the strength from her limbs, and she staggered back a step.

Walt had been her mentor and surrogate father. At eighteen, she had been living in Florida when she witnessed a murder. She'd turned state's evidence and become one of the youngest people ever relocated by the Witness Security Program.

She'd been an adult according to the law of the state if not in her heart. In her heart, she'd still been a scared kid, hoping her life might turn around once she grew up. WITSEC had taken her input seriously and placed her in Alaska. She'd never seen snow, and the most time she'd spent outdoors had been at the beach, but Alaska was as far away from Florida as she'd been able to imagine at the time—and that was good enough.

Her handler had taken her love of animals into account and secured her a job working with Walt and his sled dogs at Denali State Park. His efforts had gifted her with the most profound blessing of her life. She didn't know what would have happened if she hadn't been given that job with Walt.

He'd worked for the Witness Security Program before returning home to his beloved Alaska, and he was the only person who knew the truth about her. Good thing, too. Following her initial orientation and training, joining the WITSEC program had been little more than a glorified plane ticket out of Florida. Once they'd relocated her, she'd had very little contact with anyone in the program.

With Walt's encouragement, she'd imagined a better future for herself. He'd helped her enroll in college, and he'd kept her spirits buoyed during the years she studied veterinary medicine in the lower forty-eight. When she finally graduated, he'd helped her get her first job.

He'd been everything to her...

Walt didn't have an enemy in the world.

A horrifying suspicion took shape in her mind. If this had something to do with her, why now? Nick Amato, the man she'd seen commit a heinous murder, had died in jail six months ago. Even if someone cared enough to track her down after all these years, why come for Walt instead of her? She was an easier target.

A sound caught her attention, and she whipped around. The knob on the front door turned. Her knees went weak.

The killer had returned.

Alaska state trooper Shane Taylor concentrated on the road. Visibility was less than ten feet, and the temperature was well below zero. Gusts of wind sent sheets of snow slithering across the highway.

His four-wheel drive, extended-cab truck, though old, was equipped with a plow, a winch, a tow bar and enough emergency supplies for a week. In the dead of winter, sometimes even that wasn't enough.

A car in the ditch snagged his attention. After pulling to the side of the road, he tromped through the growing drifts and swiped a clean spot on the driver's side window. Empty. He wrapped a length of yellow police tape around the side mirror to signal the car had been checked for passengers.

Back inside his truck, he pressed his gloved hands against the warm air blowing from the vents. He was reaching for his radio when his phone caught his attention. *Kara.* His heart did a little flip-flop, and he dropped his hand to his knee.

It had been three months since she'd broken up with him. Though he knew it was for the best, his emotions still stung.

He couldn't recall ever dating anyone who'd tangled him up quite like Kara. He'd known from the beginning they were wrong for each other. She was a *cheechako*— an outsider. People like Kara came to Alaska hoping they could hide from whatever troubles they were running from in the lower forty-eight. Eventually, they all arrived at the same conclusion—even Alaska wasn't big enough that you could hide from yourself.

Shane was fiercely protective of the little community surrounding Kodiak Springs, and every instinct in his body had warned him that whatever baggage she was hiding risked the peace of his town.

Why, then, did even the sight of her name on his phone send his heart beating like a teenager with his first crush?

He pinched off his glove and swiped at the screen. The time stamp indicated the text had been sent about the time he'd spotted the car in the ditch.

Walt shot. Gunman in his house. Hiding. Sorry. For everything.

Shane quickly read the text again, his brain struggling to comprehend what he was seeing. Was he being pranked? Had someone gotten hold of Kara's phone? He read the last line again.

Sorry. For everything.

A chill pricked the hairs on the back of his neck.

This wasn't a prank.

With one last glance at Walt, Kara sprinted toward the back door. Her heavy boots skated over the slick tiles and she cracked her shin against a chair. Ignoring the stab of pain, she yanked open the back door to a frigid blast of icy snow. A pop sounded. The doorjamb splintered near her head.

Ducking left, she bolted outside. The cold hit her lungs with a painful burn, and her eyes watered. Walt usually kept the path to the kennels clear, but at least an inch of snow had already fallen this morning. Another gunshot sounded. She added a burst of speed.

Sitka and Zoya, Walt's sled dogs, barked at the commotion, and her footsteps faltered. *No.* She couldn't stop. She'd get help and return later.

Her feet skidded out from beneath her and she tumbled around the corner of the kennels. Scrambling upright, she sprinted toward her snow machine.

Not daring to look back just yet, she leaped onto the seat, turned the key, then yanked the starter. The engine roared to life. Leaning forward, she twisted the throttle. The skis caught traction and sent a plume of snow streaming behind her.

Along with the blowing snow, the trees surrounding Walt's house provided cover. She had a head start. She also had the added advantage of knowing the trail by heart. Much to Walt's horror, she'd even made the trip in the dark on one occasion.

She maneuvered around a tall spruce before glancing over her shoulder. *Nothing.* The house and the kennels had disappeared into the blizzard. No one appeared through the heavy snow.

As relief shuddered through her, a searing pain ripped across her upper thigh.

Her grip loosened. The skis swerved. The snow machine veered and flipped. Unable to right herself, she sailed through the air and landed hard on her back. The breath whooshed from her lungs.

As she struggled to rise, a wave of nausea crashed over her. She gasped for air and touched the spot on her thigh. Her hand came away smeared red.

She'd been shot.

Collapsing onto her back once more, she blinked the

melting flakes from her eyelashes. A part of her was tempted to simply close her eyes.

She fumbled for her phone, the air feeling dense around her, as though she was swimming through a thick gel. Even the simplest task felt unmanageable. Her hands ached. In her panic, she'd left her gloves behind.

She groggily raised the phone into her line of vision. No reception.

That figured. Storms around here had a way of messing with the signal.

Her arm dropped to her side. What next?

Given the temperature and the wind chill, she was at risk for frostbite and hypothermia in less than twenty minutes. But if the killer was still tracking her, the cold was the least of her worries. She had to think logically. She wasn't helpless. Not completely.

Walt deserved better. She was the only witness to his murder. She was the best chance to find his killer.

Angry flurries whipped through the pine needles, and the icy chill penetrated her snowsuit. Despite her resolve, her concentration slipped. For years after moving north, she'd still thought of Florida as her home. There'd been a part of her that even believed she might return someday.

Not anymore.

Alaska was her home now.

Alaska was where she'd been reborn, and Alaska was where she was going to die.

Just not today, God willing.

The cold seemed to abate, and her thoughts drifted to Walt.

He was home now, with his Savior. He was at rest. He was at peace.

Once he'd told her that he hoped he got to pick his age

in heaven. He wanted to be a ten-year-old boy again, and full of wonder. *That's the only thing I regret about growing old*, he'd said, *the loss of wonder.*

The tips of the pine trees arced overhead, framing the dense, gray of the falling snow. She imagined the plume of smoke rising from Walt's chimney, and her throat closed. She'd never again be greeted by the sight.

Summoning one last burst of strength, she pushed herself to her knees. She prayed that Shane might find her before it was too late, but her vision wavered and blurred.

If someone wanted her dead, however, she wasn't going down without a fight.

TWO

Shane typed quickly.

Stay in hiding. Help on the way. Don't come out for anyone but me.

He hesitated. Had Kara turned off the sound on her phone? Taking the chance, he sent the text. She was smart. She'd know what to do.

Precious minutes had passed already. *How long had she been alone with a killer?*

His training kicked in and he went through the familiar steps with methodical precision. He hit the lights and siren before radioing in his location along with the current description of the situation.

He was Sergeant Capital T Taylor now. That's what Kara used to call him when he donned his uniform. She said it was like watching someone flip a switch on his personality—and not in a good way. She barely spoke to him when he was in uniform, and only warmed up again when he changed back to his civilian clothing.

She'd never understood that when she rejected the uniform, she was rejecting *him*. Being a trooper was the only thing he'd ever been truly good at.

Even with the hazardous conditions, he drove the distance in less than fifteen minutes and exited the truck with his weapon drawn. There was no other vehicle in sight. The killer hadn't walked here in this weather, which meant he'd already fled the scene.

The temperature was still dropping, so Shane left the key in the ignition. The only way to guarantee the truck would start again was to leave it running.

Walt's house was an A-frame cabin featuring a long, shallow porch across the front. Shane peered in the window, and his pulse spiked.

Walt lay sprawled on the living room floor, a growing pool of red surrounding his body.

Kara. Had Walt's killer discovered her hiding place?

Shouting, "Alaska state trooper," he entered through the unlocked front door and searched his immediate surroundings. The house was chopped up into smaller rooms, limiting his line of sight.

He dropped to one knee beside Walt's body and checked the prone man's wrist with two fingers. No pulse.

He stalked through the kitchen and into the bedroom off the hallway where he yanked open the closet. The space was a jumble of clothes and shoes. No Kara.

He stepped back into the hallway and glanced down. Wet ovals ended at the mat near the back door. There was a second door to his right. Keeping his body angled and his gun at the ready, he whipped open the door, then rummaged through the hanging coats. Nothing. There was no place else to hide in the small house.

As he calculated his next move, her scent teased his senses, immediately triggering his emotions. He recognized the perfume Kara wore, something with cherry blossoms, she'd said.

This was where she'd hidden.

Forcing the panic from his system, Shane radioed confirmation of the homicide to the safety officer at the trooper post.

Hoping for the best but preparing for the worst, he requested backup and an ambulance.

At least there was no sign of a struggle. That boded well for Kara.

"Think, Shane," he muttered into the silence.

The kennels.

Kara put more stock in animals than people. In this case, she might have a point. Moving swiftly, Shane exited the house and bent his head into the blowing snow. Once inside the kennels, the dogs barked at his arrival. It didn't take him long to find what he needed. He snatched a leash off the hook and attached it to the collar of Walt's prize malamute.

"C'mon, Sitka." He patted the dog's head. "You're going to help me."

Sitka's ears swiveled forward.

"Right," Shane muttered.

After a hasty search, he discovered a pair of women's gloves sitting atop Kara's veterinary bag and waved them beneath the dog's nose.

Though Sitka wasn't trained in tracking, the malamute was incredibly intelligent. He'd figure it out.

"Help me," Shane cajoled. "Let's find Kara. C'mon. Just tell me which way she went, and I'll take it from there."

The dog whimpered and scuffed at the floor. Sitka lowered his head and sniffed, then made for the door.

"That's my boy!" Shane exclaimed.

Together they plunged into the blowing snow. Shane

had seen just about every disastrous outcome possible in this weather over the years.

If Kara was in this blizzard, she didn't have much time before hypothermia set in.

If there was one constant about Kara, though, she was a survivor. He'd cling to that knowledge.

Sitka took off in one direction, then hesitated, his snout kicking up tufts of snow. Shane searched for any sign of Kara's movements, but the wind had swept away any remnants of tracks. He quickly scrolled mentally through the possibilities.

Her car hadn't been parked out front, and her snow machine was nowhere to be seen. If she'd gotten to transportation, she'd be headed for town.

Sitka barked and yanked on the lead.

Shane gave the dog his head.

Feeling a tenuous thread of hope, Shane thrashed to keep up. Sitka bounded through the undulating drifts in excited leaps.

The overturned snow machine caught his attention first, and his heart stalled. Another dark form took shape through the swirling flakes. He ripped the flaps of his hat loose from around his face and gave an involuntary shout. He'd found Kara.

He looped Sitka's leash over a low branch. "Stay."

With equal amounts of hope and dread, Shane took exaggerated steps through the deepening snow.

He sank onto his knees and did a quick search for signs of injury. His rushed inspection revealed a tear in her snowsuit where blood oozed from her thigh. The wound wasn't deep, but the bleeding was worrisome.

Kara's eyes fluttered open. Her dark hair framed her

pale face, and crystalline flakes coated her long eyelashes.

He gently pressed her bare fingers between his gloved hands, and she winced.

"We'll get you squared away," he said gruffly. "Don't worry."

"Walt." Her voice was weak and barely audible over the wind. "He's—"

"I know. Don't think about that now. We have to get you back to town."

"He's, he's…"

"Are you hurt anywhere else?"

She moved her head from side to side.

"Good," he replied, infusing his voice with more optimism than he felt.

The color of the skin on her fingers indicated early stages of frostbite. He reached for the first aid kit attached to his duty belt and fumbled for a roll of bandages.

"You came for me," she said.

The note of surprise in her voice cut him to the quick.

There were times when they were dating when he'd felt as though she was looking for a reason to be disappointed in him.

This felt like one of those times. "Of course, I came."

She'd immediately snagged his eye when she'd moved to town. New people were always a novelty—but it had been more than that. There was something about Kara that had attracted him right away.

Initially, she'd been guarded. He'd been patient. Men outnumbered women in Alaska, and the attention was often overwhelming. Not wanting to upset her, he'd kept his distance at first. He'd wanted her to know he was sincere. When he'd asked her out for coffee, he'd been shocked when she said yes.

After she applied to rent one of the town houses in Kodiak Springs, he'd done a courtesy background check on her for the rental agency. There'd been nothing of note in her past. College in the lower forty-eight, then vet school. No arrests listed. Nothing out of order. That should have been enough to satisfy his curiosity. Yet after dating her for nearly four months, he'd gotten little additional information.

Her reluctance to share even the most straightforward personal details of her past set off alarm bells. She was hiding something. Soon he'd found himself waiting for the reveal with increasing dread. He'd issued an ultimatum. She'd refused to concede. End of story.

A growing pool of red saturated the snow, diluting as it seeped away, turning the crystals pink around the edges. His temporary bandage was already soaked through. He considered a tourniquet then discarded the idea. She'd lose the leg if he cut off the blood supply for too long.

"How are you doing?" he asked, raising his voice over the howling wind.

She offered a weak thumbs-up.

He peeled off his gloves and worked them over her hands. Her feeble attempt to refuse his offering worried him more than anything else.

She was lethargic and her pulse was weak. Early signs of hypothermia.

He reached for his radio, and the line crackled.

"Where's my backup and that ambulance?"

"I'm working on it." Jeff, the public safety officer who manned the desk at the trooper post, replied. More static sounded. "There's a truck jackknifed. Traffic's backed up for half a mile in both directions. It'll be an hour at least. They're closing the highway until tomorrow. The chopper won't go up in this wind."

The chopper wouldn't be much use anyway; there were too many trees surrounding Walt's house. There was no place to land.

Shane swiped the back of his hand over his forehead. "What's the current avalanche warning for the Da'nai Pass?"

The line crackled. "Chugach National Forest Avalanche Center says the snowpack is unstable. No travel recommended."

Some days a guy caught all the breaks, and some days he didn't. "Cancel the backup. With this wind, that snowpack is going to give. Close the exit to the Kodiak Springs Resort for the next twelve hours."

The service road to the resort T-boned off the highway. Walt's drive was about a half mile off the exit. After that, the road wound its way nearly five miles to the resort, through an area that passed straight through the Da'nai Valley. The area was a perfect avalanche chute. As often as twice a year, the snowpack broke loose and covered the road. They'd had no fatalities as of yet, and Shane wanted to keep it that way. He already had one body on his hands.

"What's your plan?" Jeff asked.

"Get a forensics team up here as soon as you can. I'll try and secure the scene."

If he took Kara to the resort, he risked being caught on the wrong side of the pass if the snowpack broke loose. If he tried to make it back to town, he risked Kara bleeding out before he reached the medical center. Without knowing the extent of her injuries, he had to err on the side of caution.

A memory tugged at the back of Shane's brain. The resort catered to the wealthy, and he'd seen a familiar face at the café in town.

He depressed the call button. "There's a surgeon staying at the hot springs. I'll take Dr. Riley there. We'll reassess first thing in the morning."

"Hot springs...reroute."

Jeff's message cut out. Shane muttered beneath his breath. Radio contact was tricky in the mountains in the best of conditions. Sitka pawed at the snow. Shane couldn't hold the leash and carry Kara. He'd have to trust the dog's intelligence.

"Time to go back to the kennels," he said, unhooking the leash.

The dog bounded ahead without a backward glance. Sitka knew the way, all right.

With Kara in his arms, Shane surged to his feet.

He'd have to work quickly. Kara had been shot, Walt was dead and Shane risked being trapped on the wrong side of the pass with a killer on the loose.

Kara was blissfully numb. At least she was no longer cold. Part of her knew that was bad. She was experiencing the classic signs of hypothermia. The other part of her didn't care. She only wanted to sleep.

Her head jostled and she opened her eyes. "Shane."

He'd come for her. She'd never doubted he would. Though they'd ended their relationship on a sour note, she trusted Sergeant Capital T Taylor in an emergency. He was fiercely protective of his town.

The wind whipped over her and snowflakes blurred

her vision. Her head was gradually clearing, and the pain roared to life.

She must have made a noise because Shane glanced down. "Are you all right? It's not much farther to the house."

"We have to get the dogs."

"They're fine. Sitka practically opened the door to the kennels himself. You should be worried about yourself."

"It's not too bad."

"Listen, let's get you out of this weather, then I can worry about the dogs."

"I guess."

His coat made his shoulders look even broader, and his beard had filled in. When she'd arrived during the warmer summer months, he'd been clean shaven. As winter approached, he'd grown the beard. She liked it.

"The cold helped," he said, his voice sounding odd. "Doesn't look like you've suffered too much blood loss, but we need to get you medical attention."

Walt's house appeared through the blizzard winds, and her eyes burned. "What if you can't make it back? The puppies can't be left alone."

"Then I'll figure something else out."

His abrupt dismissal raised her hackles. This was the Shane she'd broken up with—the stubborn, implacable sergeant. She'd known he was a state trooper when he asked her out, but she'd said yes anyway.

At first, she'd thought the invitation was some sort of initiation. *Who could date the new girl first?* Turned out, he'd been genuinely interested in her. A terrifying realization.

She blamed Sitka for the whole mess. The sled dog had taken an instant liking to him, and Kara always trusted animals over people. Not to mention the fact that Shane's sky blue uniform with its wide-brimmed hat was a far cry from the uniforms the Anchorage police wore. Even the sight of one of those uniforms on the news brought back disturbing memories.

Because her mom tended to operate on the wrong side of the law, Kara hadn't had many positive encounters with law enforcement growing up.

Turned out the design of the uniform didn't matter. Whenever Shane was dressed for duty, she felt nervous and powerless.

Not to mention, dating him was dangerous if she wanted to keep her past hidden. He had an instinct for lies, and he must have sensed something about her didn't quite add up.

He'd slip into the professional habits she recognized from when the social workers called the police on her mom. Whether it was an argument between her mom and her mom's current boyfriend, complaints from the neighbors, or yet another drug charge, the police were frequent, unwelcome visitors.

Shane was well-versed in all the techniques. He'd ask her the same question over and over again in different ways. Then he'd come at the question from a different angle. Anything to trip her up in a lie. He couldn't leave well enough alone.

He'd forewarned her that if she wasn't willing to contribute more to the relationship—to him—then maybe they shouldn't be together. She'd called his ultimatum. That was the last time she'd spoken to him before today.

Her chest squeezed. Turned out dogs couldn't be trusted to pick romantic partners, and the color of the uniform didn't matter as much as the uniform itself.

They arrived at the truck and Shane set her gently on her feet.

He reached for the door. "I'm taking you to the hot springs. There's a surgeon there."

"I don't need a surgeon. The medical clinic in town is close enough."

"Highway is closed," Shane replied. "And we need to move quickly. There's an avalanche alert."

To his credit, not a muscle in his jaw twitched. Their last disagreement had been about the road to the hot springs. A generation before, Walt's family had feuded with Shane's family over who owned the property where the hot springs were located. Shane's family eventually won the dispute and promptly started construction of a rustic hotel that eventually morphed into a compact luxury resort and spa.

Furious over the decision, Walt's family managed to scrape together enough money to buy a parcel of land on the ridge overlooking the hot spring that included the easement needed to build a road. The resort had been forced to reroute access through the treacherous Da'nai Valley, instead.

The feud had been a source of dysfunction in the town for sixty years. Walt's return to the property had stirred up the bad blood once more, but he wasn't selling. Walt was a patient and even-tempered man, and an offer from the resort to buy the land had infuriated him. That had been the only time she'd ever seen him angry.

Shane had tried to talk her into speaking with him about allowing the easement, and she'd refused. A teeth-clenching argument had ensued.

Shane leaned over her, reaching toward the steering wheel.

He made a sound of frustration and retracted his hand. "What's wrong?"

"Get down," he ordered harshly. "Someone took the keys."

The chill in her blood came rushing back. In Alaska, people left their cars running. It was a matter of survival.

Crouching, he reached beneath the fender and pulled out a magnetic key holder. He slid open the lid. The container was empty.

Staying low, Shane circled the truck and scooted into the driver's seat, then bent over her. "There was no vehicle when I got here, which means the killer must have hidden a snow machine in the woods. That narrows down our search parameters."

"If he took the keys, he's still out there."

"Or he's slowing us down while he escapes. I should have known better than to leave the keys. It's a habit."

"Has anyone ever stolen a police vehicle in Kodiak Springs?"

"Are you kidding? I doubt I could pay someone to steal this thing."

She met his steady gaze, their faces inches apart. Close enough that she could count his eyelashes one by one if she'd been so inclined. Why was it that men always seemed to get the beautiful eyelashes? And why had such a random thought entered her head during a life-and-death situation? She must be worse off than she thought.

"Maybe he thinks I can identify him," she said.

"Can you?"

"No." She considered the past forty minutes. "Something must have tipped him off that I was there. He came back."

Shane's hands tightened on her shoulders. "You got away. That's what matters."

"What are we going to do now?"

Fear rattled in her chest and her mind blanked. She clung to the tenuous control she'd gained since Shane's arrival, though a part of her hated it, hated herself for craving his warmth and his safety. She didn't want to depend on anyone but herself and God for strength.

Closing her eyes, she murmured, "'The Lord is my light and my salvation. Whom shall I fear? The Lord is the stronghold of my life; of whom shall I be afraid?'"

"Amen," Shane said softly. He inched a little higher and peered over the dash. "I still don't see anything."

A pop sounded and a plume of snow exploded into the air near the driver's side fender. Kara shrieked and reached for Shane, clinging to him. Terror clawed at her chest. It was easy to tell herself to have faith and so hard to do when tested.

"He doesn't want a head start." Kara's heart thudded painfully against her ribs. "He wants to kill us."

THREE

Kara was frozen in terror. If Walt's death had been because of her, then she risked two lives. Shane was in the line of fire with her.

A flash of light caught her attention.

She covered her head. Shane draped his body protectively over hers.

A bullet ricocheted off the front fender with a metallic thud.

"Stay down," Shane whispered harshly.

"Don't worry. I'm too scared to move." Her breath came in quick, shallow gasps. "We're trapped here."

His weight eased. "I'm taking care of this guy. We're sitting ducks."

"No." She clutched his arm. "You can't go out there. You don't know where he is. You could walk right into a bullet."

"I'm not letting him get to you."

"It's too dangerous."

"Then we'll freeze to death." Shane straightened slightly and slipped his gun from his holster. "We can't just sit here."

"If he kills you, we're both dead," she whispered.

He dropped his hand with a sigh. Both of them braced for another bullet, but none came. Shane reached for his radio and called dispatch. Nothing but static met his plea.

He replaced the mic. "Great."

Kara's back ached from the awkward position, and her leg throbbed. Her heart was pounding hard enough to make her chest burn.

Shane was right about one thing. Waiting for the killer to come to them was a poor option.

Her eyes were level with the gearshift, and an idea took shape. Jack, the man whose murder she'd witnessed, had been a repo man. She'd worked for him that summer, and there was a little-known trick in the business she'd learned when he took her out on one of his runs.

"This drive is steep." She spoke her thoughts aloud. "Real steep."

"Yep."

"That means if we can get the truck into neutral, we can roll backward."

"In theory. But we'll have no power steering, no brakes and visibility is next to nil."

"The farther we are away, the more difficult we are to target."

"Yeah." Shane's brow creased. "How much time does that buy us?"

She gestured vaguely toward the house. "This guy knows we'll eventually have to leave the truck. Our only choices are the house or the kennels. I think that's why his shots are so far apart. He's trying to lure us into making a run for it. What he's not expecting is for the truck to move backward."

He turned his attention to her. "True."

This just might work. "The hot springs snowplow will

start running as soon as the blizzard lets up. We can flag down the driver."

"That might be a long wait. Especially if the avalanche warning stays in effect."

Kara shrugged. "I'll take a better idea."

Her side mirror exploded. She might have screamed; she didn't know. Shane pressed her farther down, crushing her injured leg. The pain barely registered. Her fear was sharper than anything else that was happening.

He hunched forward and grasped her fingers with his free hand. "On second thought, let's make for the road and hope the snow passes soon."

His hand was warm and strong, and for a moment she was sheltered in his strength. This time she didn't fight the comfort. Maybe, just this once, it was okay to lean on someone.

"This is going to work," she said.

He dropped his hold on her and swiveled awkwardly in his seat. "Seat belts. This isn't going to be smooth."

She reached for the belt and tugged. Shane leaned over and covered her trembling hand with his, guiding the metal tongue into the latch with a click. As he did the same for himself, she stared at the junction. The almost paternal gesture yanked her momentarily back to her childhood. Though she knew someone must have, she didn't recall anyone ever buckling her in.

Shane cracked the door and fired off a shot. "That'll keep him busy while we figure this out."

Echoes of the gunshot set her ears ringing, making his voice sound tinny and distant. Even in the freezing temperatures, a chill sweat broke out on her forehead. The cold and the shock were beginning to wear on her.

"There's one flaw in the plan." Shane yanked on the

gearshift. "This truck is well-outfitted, but it's ancient. I don't know if I can wrestle it into neutral."

If he questioned her later, she'd tell him she'd seen the trick in a movie or something. "I know what to do."

Shane had questions, but knowing better than to ask, he kept his own counsel. "What do you need?"

"A screwdriver," she said. "The smaller the better."

"Got it." A quick rummage revealed a medium-size screwdriver. "Will this do?"

"Perfect."

Her brow knitted, Kara pried open a tiny plastic cover near the gearshift, then pressed her finger through the opening. "All right. Drop it into neutral."

To his surprise, the gear shift easily slid into place. The truck jolted but didn't move. He'd learned a lot of tricks about cars over the years, but that was a new one.

Seconds ticked by. An almost imperceptible movement vibrated through the wheels. The truck slowly inched backward.

"You know your stuff," he said, glancing over his shoulder in a rapid up and down movement.

His sight line was poor, which meant judging the turn was going to be tricky.

Kara grimaced. "I don't know. We're barely moving."

"Give it a minute," he said, his back hunched. "Gravity will take over. When I was a kid, I accidentally kicked my mom's car into neutral climbing over the seat."

"What happened? Did you get hurt?"

"Nah. Crashed into the neighbor's fence."

Maybe the shooter wouldn't notice they were moving right away. That might buy them a precious few seconds.

Snow flurries whipped across the windshield. Despite

his reassurances, Shane's pulse thudded. As he held his breath, the truck gradually picked up speed.

All his doubts about the plan came rushing back.

He lifted his head slightly. "This isn't going to be easy, the steering is electric." With one hand on her shoulder, he kept his body angled over hers, the other hand clutching the wheel. "Given visibility, we'll be taking the turn blind."

"At least we're moving." Kara angled her head. "We might actually make it."

He prayed she was right. He didn't think it was possible, but her face had grown even paler. First things first. He'd worry about what to do next as soon as they were out of the killer's range.

Shane reluctantly scooted away, removing his hand from Kara's shoulder. "Brace yourself and stay down. This might get rough."

He didn't dare lift his head any higher than the top of the steering wheel. There was no mistaking the movement now. How aggressively was the gunman prepared to chase them? How much firepower did he have?

Shane calculated the distance to the bend in the middle of Walt's long drive. He'd have to angle the wheels early if he was going to make it. Though he'd been to Walt's house a few times over the years, he hadn't exactly memorized the terrain. He recalled a copse of trees in the bend of the drive and a deep trench on either side of it right before the highway.

The wheels bumped over the snowy surface. He counted to three and risked lifting his head enough to peer at the rearview mirror.

A dark shape caught his attention. He yanked on the

wheel and the tires angled. The truck skidded. Another couple of feet and they might have made it.

"Hang on!" he hollered.

The sickening crunch of metal striking one of the tall pines echoed through the canyon. The impact yanked the wheel from his hands, and his neck snapped back. The steep grade and icy conditions kept the weight of the truck sliding. The front wheels skidded, propelling them sideways down the hill.

Shane wrestled with the steering wheel, wrenching as hard as he could, but with no traction, the bed of the truck swung around as though it was trying to pass them. Another glancing blow sent them fishtailing.

Even if he'd had more control over the steering, he doubted he'd be able to maneuver in these conditions. The brakes were worthless and the truck was picking up speed again.

Unless he corrected their trajectory, they were going to hit the ditch.

The front wheels glided over the icy drive, and they hydroplaned in slow motion.

He glanced to his right and his heart stalled. The break in the trees indicated they were nearing the road. If they hit the ditch at this speed, the way they were angled, they'd flip.

The truck had become a six-thousand-pound out-of-control battering ram headed straight for the disaster.

FOUR

Kara instinctively covered her head and cringed.

Papers careened off the dash and part of the police radio broke loose. For a crystalline moment, time seemed to slow. She watched with detached interest as an empty paper cup sailed through the air. A column of snow, kicked up from the skidding tires, arced gracefully over the windshield.

Her elbow banged against the dash and pain radiated through her arm. In an instant time sped up. The truck pitched sideways. She frantically groped for anything to stabilize herself against the painful battering. Just when she thought they might flip, the truck righted itself with a sickening thud.

Her teeth slammed together, and her head cracked against the side window. Agony exploded from her toes to her thigh.

She might have blacked out for a minute. She wasn't certain. Afraid to trust in the sudden silence, she remained motionless for an agonizing beat.

Shane dragged himself upright using the steering wheel. "Are you hurt?"

She gave herself a quick pat down as though her hands

might discover an injury before her brain acknowledged the pain.

Kara shook her head. "No new injuries. Just shaken up."

She'd been in a state of unrelenting panic for the past hour, and the eerie calm was unsettling.

A dense whiteout cocooned them, muffling the exterior noises. There was nothing but blank space beyond the ten-foot radius surrounding the truck. It was like one of those movie scenes where the character enters an endless, blank void.

She wasn't even certain which direction they were facing. There was no way to tell. There were no landmarks to judge her bearings.

Both of them remained alert, searching for any sign of an impending attack.

"Do you see anything?" Kara asked in a low whisper.

"Nothing."

He scooted down and pressed a lever, shoving the seat back as far as it would go. Kara followed his lead. They used the extra space to crouch low. A feat that was far easier for her to manage. Shane barely fit. There was no way to switch positions just yet, leaving him to battle the steering wheel and the column.

He fumbled for the radio and reattached one of the wires. He tried to make a call, but there was no reply. Static sounded, which meant there was no way to know if the radio was broken or if the storm was interfering with the reception. They both instinctively reached for their phones. Neither of them had any bars. They exchanged a glance, saying nothing, yet both conveying the paralyzing uncertainty of their current situation. He pushed his flapped hat back from his forehead, smearing blood across his temple.

Kara gasped. "You're hurt!"

He swiped at the spot. "I'm not good with blood. Especially my own."

She flashed a half grin despite herself. "You're joshing me. You patched me up just fine."

This was the part of being an adult she'd never quite mastered. Should she offer to help him? Ask him if he needed a Band-Aid? She knew what to do when an animal was hurt or in pain; she wasn't so certain about people.

"Looks like I've got you fooled," he said.

She adjusted her leg and winced.

When she straightened, her head swam. "It's weird. I feel like we're still moving."

"We took a good hit," he said. "It'll pass." He patted the dash affectionately. "At least the department will finally qualify for an updated vehicle. This one had seen better days five years ago."

The conversation was forced, with Shane trying to assume an air of normalcy to alleviate the terror, and her trying to process everything that had happened. How long before it was safe to venture out? At this point, there was nothing to do but wait.

"If you get any say about the new truck, make sure it has a key fob this time around," she said. "Come to think of it, do they even make cars that use keys anymore?"

He snorted at the good-natured ribbing. "It's my fault. Bill, one of the safety officers, loses his keys every other week. I should have checked to make sure he put the spare key back."

Her own car was ancient. She was still paying off her

student loans, which meant it'd be a while before she replaced it.

"I don't think anyone could have planned for what happened," she said. "You can't blame yourself."

From his expression, she surmised that he could, and he would, blame himself no matter how many words of consolation she provided.

Her legs tingled with pins and needles. She shifted, and a stinging pain ran from her wounded thigh to her foot.

With a grimace, Kara started to rise.

Shane flashed his palm. "I don't trust this guy. He isn't behaving normally. Most killers don't stick around once the police arrive."

Her teeth chattered. "Do you really think he's still out there?"

"He's somewhere." Shane narrowed his gaze at the emptiness outside the windshield. "Depends on how badly he wants us."

The pins and needles were traveling up her calves. "For all he knows, you did have another set of keys. Maybe he thinks we're long gone by now."

"Let's hope so." Shane swiveled in his seat, then stretched his arm and grasped his shotgun from the rack. "But we'd better plan for the worst. You know how to use this?"

The wooden stock was smooth and cold against her bare fingers. "Well enough."

Gun safety was one of the first things Walt had taught her. She'd initially resisted his insistence that she learn how to shoot. She'd already seen too much violence in her life. Even the sight of a gun brought back memories she'd prefer to forget.

Walt had persisted. He'd gradually worn down her defenses with his calm, steady example. In Alaska, guns were survival. They were a tool, the same as an ax or a shovel.

"There's one shell in the chamber and two in the magazine," Shane said. "Be careful."

"I know." Emotion tightened her throat, and she checked the safety mechanism. "I was taught by the best."

The last two words were barely more than a squeak.

Shane tenderly cupped the back of her head with his enormous hand. "I know this is hard. You're holding up great. I promise when this is over, you can mourn properly for Walt."

She allowed herself a moment of weakness before leaning away. "Sure."

He removed his hand, though the warmth of his touch lingered.

Keeping her face averted, she swiped her nose against her sleeve.

Only two weeks ago, she and Walt had traveled the south border of his property searching for a wounded wolf he'd seen earlier. There had been nothing special about that day. Nothing to mark that it would be the last time they tackled the outdoors together.

Walt had talked about the new litter of puppies. He'd even promised to give her one as a Christmas present. She'd protested. Her job was unpredictable, and the hours were long. She took care of enough dogs already.

Walt had only smiled. He knew she had a soft spot for Christmas. Her birthday was on the twenty-third of December, and people always forgot it. No one ever forgot Christmas.

Walt had introduced her to the Candlelight Mass. It was a tradition she and Walt shared.

Emotion threatened to overwhelm her, and she shut down the flood of memories, forcing her mind to go blank. She'd opened herself to joy, and this was the consequence. That's why it was better to feel nothing.

Using his elbow, Shane wiped a larger circle in the growing condensation. "I can't even tell if we're on the road." He depressed the call button on the police radio and static sounded. He shrugged. "It was worth a shot. Jeff is at the duty station tonight. Keep trying him. I'll be back in a few."

Her heart dropped. "Where are you going?"

The note of hysteria in her voice was lowering. She was a strong, independent woman. She simply didn't want to be alone in the wilderness with a murderer on the loose—a perfectly reasonable fear, considering her leg injury had her at a disadvantage.

"I need to get the lay of the land," Shane said, his attention focused on the fathomless abyss swirling outside the windshield. "See if I can figure out where we are in reference to the road. Then we can make a plan."

She knew him well enough to know there'd be no talking him out of the decision.

He was too stubborn. "Don't go too far."

"Don't shoot me," he replied, gesturing toward the shotgun. "I'll keep my hands up when I approach. That way, you'll know it's me."

She appreciated the extra precaution, but there was no need. She'd recognize him anywhere. In town, she could spot him from two blocks away. He had a certain purposeful intent in his walk. A confident, distinctive way of holding himself.

"Be, uh…" The words clogged in her throat.

Shutting down the pain of one loss was going to be hard enough. She didn't want to face another.

"I'll be careful," he said.

The look in his expressive blue eyes might have been regret.

She wasn't stupid. This was her cue. This was her chance to say something—to start mending the rift between them.

No words came. Why expose an old wound? They were wrong for each other. She had secrets to protect and keeping them from Shane had drained the life from her. He was relentless. He'd sensed a snag in the fabric of her life, and he wouldn't be satisfied until he pulled the thread. She refused to let that happen. Anyone who knew about her past was in danger.

"How long will you be gone?" was all she managed to say.

"I'm not sure." He paused, his gaze intense, and she shrank away from his scrutiny. "Keep trying to reach Jeff," he continued. "Check your phone for bars, as well. The mountains can be tricky. If I don't come back, don't come looking for me. There's food and blankets. You've got enough supplies to wait out the storm. Jeff is smart. If he doesn't hear from us, he'll send someone from the resort out looking."

If anyone was crazy enough to go out in this storm, that person was most likely from Alaska. Though weather this bad was rare, it was not unheard-of. Not to mention the unpredictability. Blizzards that were supposed to bury towns petered out, and storms that were supposed to blow over exploded into bomb cyclones. For all they knew, this whole thing might be over in another hour.

"If you're determined to put yourself in harm's way—" she pinched off the gloves he'd placed on her hands earlier "—you'll need these."

After reluctantly conceding the point, he rummaged around in the back seat once more. "Here's a blanket. This should help keep you warm."

"It's not too late to reconsider," she blurted, immediately regretting the lapse.

People did what they wanted to do. He wasn't going to stick around just because she asked.

"I need to get my bearings," he said. "If we're sitting in the middle of the road, I'll have to put out reflectors when the storm breaks. I don't want to survive this only to be crushed by a snowplow."

He had a point, but he was still putting himself at risk.

While she recognized any sense of security that she felt in the truck was false, the idea of separating had her panicked. They were less than half a football field away from the house, but it might as well have been a mile. There was nothing but a sea of white surrounding them. There was no telling who was hiding in that whiteout.

"I mean it," Shane said, his voice low and firm. "If I don't come back, don't come looking for me."

She gave a mock salute. "Got it, Sergeant Capital T Taylor."

She was already embarrassed that she'd asked him to stay. There was no point in further humiliating herself.

A shadow she didn't understand passed through his eyes. "Keep trying to reach Jeff."

She nodded. "I will."

The door opened with a shock of frigid air and churning snowflakes before he slammed it once more, entombing her in silence. If she had to be stranded with someone, she was grateful it was Shane.

He wasn't simply a part of Kodiak Springs, though he was certainly an integral member of the town. He was a part of the fabric of the land itself. He carried himself naturally in any situation, and she'd never seen him flustered. He managed the bar fights on Friday nights with the same calm, steady demeanor he used when meeting with the bereaved.

Since the town had such a small law enforcement presence, he was often tasked with being counselor and social worker to people who were also his neighbors and friends. He remained steadfast throughout it all. There had been times when she was jealous of his ability to navigate such disparate situations.

He never seemed ill at ease, while she constantly battled against feeling out of place. The only time she felt truly at home was when she was working with animals. She understood their behaviors. A horse that was in pain didn't try to hide it. A dog that was happy to see its owner didn't try to temper his joy. An angry bear protected her cubs. There was no subterfuge with animals. No guesswork involved.

The radio crackled.

"Call…snow…resort…highway."

Her pulse jumped.

She frantically snatched the microphone and depressed the button. "Jeff, it's Dr. Riley. We're stranded on the road at the bottom of Walt's driveway." The words tumbled from her lips and she paused to catch a breath. "Someone shot at us. When it's clear, send the snowplow from the resort."

Releasing the button, she waited for a reply.

"Wait…you are…out."

"Can you repeat that?"

"Order…delayed."

She made a sound of frustration. There was no way of knowing whether or not he'd heard anything she'd said.

Fumbling for her phone, she checked the bars for the umpteenth time. Still nothing. Her leg throbbed and she flashed back to the shooting. Even with snow looming in the forecast, when she'd awoken that morning the weather had been beautiful. Clear and crisp and bright enough to blind her. The dark clouds had descended rapidly and she'd felt the first wet flakes on her cheeks before she reached Walt's. While tending to the pups, she'd lost track of time. Stepping outside once more had been a shock. As long as she'd lived in Alaska, she'd never quite grown accustomed to how quickly conditions changed.

A gust of wind rattled the truck's windows, startling her. According to her phone, Shane had been gone for nearly half an hour. What was keeping him?

She adjusted the shotgun and flexed her fingers. Her hands ached from gripping the chilly gunstock.

A flash of movement in the side mirror snagged her attention. Shotgun in hand, she whipped around.

Her breath immediately fogged the glass. She swiped at the moisture and squinted. An enormous bull moose materialized through the whirling snow. He lifted his head and stared at the truck in what appeared to be mocking indifference before turning away.

Keeping low and still, she tracked his progress for as long as the blowing snow allowed. He was probably thinking, *idiot human*.

She checked the time again. Shane's gear was top-of-the-line, but in this weather, even top-of-the-line had its limits.

A soft, glowing light appeared through the haze. Her gaze sharpened. She tucked her finger into the trigger of the shotgun and squinted. A headlight, maybe? She couldn't tell. She scrunched lower in the seat and rested the barrel of the gun on the opposite window.

The light twinkled and disappeared.

There was a low rumbling, but she couldn't tell which direction the noise was coming from. She pressed one hand against her chest in an effort to slow her thumping heart.

If the killer had discovered her, she was as good as dead. There was nowhere else to run.

FIVE

Shane tapped on the window to get Kara's attention.

Good thing he did, too. The moment she heard the knocking, she shrieked and nearly dropped the gun.

He cracked the door. "Didn't mean to scare you."

"I think I saw something. A light."

"It was me," he said, reaching for the rear door handle. "I brought you something."

Sitka and Zoya automatically leaped into the back seat. He lifted the box he'd attached to the back of Walt's snow machine and slid it in beside them.

Kara exclaimed and reached over the seat.

When she turned back to him, her expression was stormy.

"You went back there."

He'd only agreed to her plan to put more distance between her and the killer before he made his move. As he stared into her butterscotch eyes, he saw the exact moment when she realized it too. He winced away from the betrayal in her gaze.

He was paid to protect his town, and that's what he planned on doing. "The killer was long gone. Didn't even find tracks. Not in this wind. I locked up the house and turned off the propane. Loaded up the puppies. Walt's snow machine was gassed up with keys in the ignition. There might be a way out tomorrow once the snow clears. The unit from Major Crimes won't be here until late tonight, or maybe even tomorrow."

Her eyes welled up and he silently chastised himself. He never seemed to get things right with Kara.

She turned around and hitched herself over the seat.

Leaning down, she reached into the box of puppies. "Thanks for getting them."

There were five squirming, soft bodies in the box. They'd been sleeping when he gathered them up.

The ground beneath his feet vibrated. He took out his binoculars and aimed them in the distance. He'd been able to calculate where they were in reference to the road. All he could see through the blowing snow was a faint glimmer from a pair of lights.

"We've got company," he said. "I see lights on the road coming from the resort. Listen, I want to keep what happened to Walt quiet for the time being. Just until the storm clears. There's nowhere to go from here, no shelter for miles outside of Walt's house and the resort. There's a good chance that's where the killer is staying. What better place to blend in if you're from out of town?"

Kara set the safety on the shotgun. "What if that's the killer coming toward us? What then?"

"It's not. Headlights are too high. The engine is too loud. It's a snowplow." He glanced over his shoulder. "We don't have much time. I'll flag them down. We'll tell the driver you had a snow machine accident."

He straightened and slammed the door. Icy pellets peppered his cheeks.

With his flashlight aimed at the snowplow, Shane

raised his free hand and waved his arm back and forth to signal the driver.

While he was fairly certain the truck had been sent for them, he wasn't taking any chances. Not with visibility this limited.

The headlights shimmered as the truck came to a halt. The door opened and a man dressed in a snowsuit and ski mask leaped from the tall seat. Shane lowered his hand to his utility belt and let his fingers hover above his weapon. There was no harm in being too careful.

The driver started toward them. His arms worked and he heaved his jutted elbows with each step through the growing snow drifts. There was nothing menacing in that approach.

When the driver reached Shane, he splayed his arms. "Hey bro, what kind of trouble did you get into now?"

Following a brief flash of shock, Shane's posture relaxed, and he lowered his flashlight to his side. "Didn't expect to see you driving a snowplow."

His stepbrother, Graham, pushed his face mask up to rest in a crumple of wool on his forehead. "I'm rusty, that's for sure. But when I heard my big brother needed help, I wasn't going to send anyone else. Especially with an avalanche warning in effect. This time *you* owe *me*."

Their relationship was amiable if not warm. Nineteen years ago, Shane had still been grieving his mom's death when his dad brought home a new wife and a new little brother. Only fifteen at the time, Shane hadn't been inclined to roll out the welcome mat. The fact that his dad had been a different man for his new family hadn't helped.

Though Shane recognized none of that was Graham's fault, there were times when he grew tired of keeping the old family secrets. Growing up, the abuse in the house had been kept behind closed doors. In public, they were a loving family. Away from prying eyes, things were different. Too young to intercede, Shane had tried to protect his mom anyway. His feeble actions had only made matters worse. He hadn't been able to protect his mother then or when she succumbed to cancer.

Two weeks after the funeral, his dad had quit drinking and things improved. Losing his wife had broken something loose inside him. But for Shane, it was too little, too late. Why hadn't his father had that epiphany before Shane's mother was gone? When she needed the love and kindness. His dad had died suddenly eighteen months ago. Heart attack. His second wife, Graham's mom, had promptly moved to California and Graham had taken over the resort. Shane sold him the twenty-five percent share he'd received from the estate and never looked back.

Graham crouched, planted his hands on his thighs and peered around Shane. "You got someone else with you?"

"Yeah," Shane replied. "The veterinarian, Doc Riley. She was transporting some sled dogs when she ran into trouble. Hurt her leg. Now the road's out."

"Well that explains why you're stuck in a blizzard and not sitting by the fire at Walt's."

"I thought maybe that surgeon staying at the resort could take a look in the meantime," Shane said.

"Dr. Lipmann? He's the best. You'd have to wait six months to get an appointment if you lived in New York."

"The sooner we get her stitched up the better."

"It's that bad?"

"Got a pretty good gash."

"Well don't stand around." Graham pivoted and

brought his arm up in an arc. "I'm freezing my nose off. Let's get out of here ASAP."

Shane circled around to the passenger side and opened the door. Kara swiveled in her seat and attempted to stand.

"Let me help," Shane said. "We'll have you warmed up in no time."

She turned her gaze toward where the house sat on the hill. Though nothing was visible through the snow, tears pooled in her eyes. Doubt ate away at him like acid. The resort was the best place to remain anonymous in a small town like Kodiak Springs. Which meant there was a chance Walt's murderer would be there, blending in with the guests. Keep everything looking normal.

Shane's arms tightened around Kara. If his intuition was correct, then he wasn't leaving her side.

Because there was a chance one of the resort guests had just committed murder.

Kara flipped off the covers and limped to the window. She'd called her assistant and informed her that she'd be out for a few days. Thankfully the clinic was slow around the holidays. She only had a few appointments she needed to cancel.

She gripped the oyster-gray silk curtains and curled her toes in the lush pile carpeting. Everything about the resort was sumptuous to the point of decadence. They'd given her a suite with a living room, dining area and separate bedroom.

This was no ordinary resort with an overly chlorinated pool and free continental breakfast. This was an exclusive, boutique resort for the wealthy. Carrera marble flanked the soaker tub and the spacious suites were dressed in cool, calming tones. The lobby featured sand-hued drapes and dove-gray furniture scattered in carefully considered groupings. The restaurant was gourmet, and breakfast was delivered with a linen napkin.

In the summer there were ATV tours and glacier dog sledding. Local guides took the wealthy on wildlife viewing adventures and kayaking trips. There was fishing and hiking and rock climbing.

From early December through March, the resort catered to a different, less adventurous crowd. Water from the hot springs was piped to an indoor pool. Some people thought the minerals in the water had healing properties. Kara figured it was the warmth that soothed their arthritis and gout, not the minerals.

The wealthy who came for the healing properties weren't concerned with science. Staying at the resort was a chance to visit the spa and enjoy the northern lights. They lazed in the waters while discreet waiters delivered drinks in crystal glasses.

Kara's skin itched as though she was allergic to the place.

Staying at the resort made her jittery. People who'd grown up poor always had certain "tells" that gave away their upbringing. She didn't have amusing anecdotes from her trips abroad to chat about over cocktails. Half the time, she didn't even understand the menu at the restaurant. The last time she'd eaten there, she'd pretended to text someone while she searched for the meaning of béchamel.

People no longer looked down on her and she liked it that way. That's why she preferred to stay in her lane. She was just a middle-class woman with a good job and piles of student loans.

She tested her leg and found it could bear weight. The whip-thin surgeon had been efficient and kind. He'd managed to drum up supplies and stitched her leg with neat precision.

When Shane told the doctor that she'd been injured in a snow machine accident, he'd raised a bushy gray eyebrow in skeptical acknowledgement. He'd known they were lying but he hadn't given them away. A consummate professional, he'd only resumed his work.

A quiet knock sounded, and she turned away from the blizzard still raging outside.

Kara limped to the door. "Who is it?"

"Shane."

Hearing his voice eased her tension. She opened the door and discovered he was wearing his parka and his boots still had fresh snow on the toes.

"The dogs are fine," he said without preamble. "They're tucked away in the kennels with the resort sled dogs."

They were in good hands. The kennels at the resort were nicer than most of the houses in town, and she knew the caretaker, Trisha, well.

Shane wadded his fur-lined hat in his hands, realized what he was doing and tossed it onto a chair. "There's nothing else I can do. The Bureau of Investigations isn't expecting a break in the weather anytime soon."

How quickly Walt had changed from a living, breathing person with a soul to nothing more than a source of evidence.

"Then you're stuck here too?" she asked, wanting to change the subject.

"Yep. Even if the snow lets up, the road isn't safe, which means we can't risk going through the pass." He rubbed the back of his neck with one hand. "I was hoping to leave tonight."

"You and me both."

She couldn't stop thinking about how he'd gone back to Walt's house. The only reason he'd even attempted her plan with the truck was because he wanted her safely out of the way before he put himself at risk. While she appreciated his concern, going back there had been dangerous. She'd already lost Walt; she couldn't face the thought of losing someone else. Didn't Shane realize how much he meant to the town? To her? Didn't he realize how much the people counted on him? Needed him?

Feeling beleaguered, she didn't hide the note of censure in her voice. "I'm still angry that you went back there. Alone. Especially after what happened." Another thought occurred to her. "Does Graham suspect the dogs belong to Walt?"

"The kennels aren't high on his list of priorities. Even if he bothered to check, I doubt he'd know the difference between Walt's dogs and the resort dogs."

"What about the highway?"

"Impassable. It's a parking lot. Bunch of big rigs had to be abandoned. They're still towing them out."

Walt's house would be freezing. Though she knew it was irrational, a part of her hated thinking of him all alone and cold.

She ducked her head against the sudden rush of tears.

Keeping her face averted, she perched on the edge of the gray love seat. The cushion depressed beside her and a comforting arm draped over her shoulder. Too drained to resist, she leaned into him, taking solace in his quiet reassurance. Shane's parka was cool against her cheek, and her tears beaded and slid down the waterproof material like melting rain drops.

A feeling stirred inside her. Something she hadn't felt

in a long time. With a pang of regret, she recognized it as longing.

Her few months with Shane had been some of the best in her life. Beneath the joy, however, a quiet sense of anxiety had infused their time together. She'd always kept her life neat and compact, never asking for too much. If she didn't let people close to her, they'd never be disappointed. She'd never even told Walt her mistakes. Not about how she'd had to retake organic chemistry or how she'd had an anxiety attack during her first surgery.

None of that had insulated her from tragedy. Walt was gone.

She shifted her head to peer at Shane, and when his gaze connected with hers, she caught a flash of something raw. The look was gone so quickly she thought she must have imagined it. His eyes broke away first.

A fresh wave of grief crashed over her, and she sought to shut down her emotions. This time, though, the skill that had served her so well in the past deserted her.

She didn't know how long they sat like that. Her quietly sobbing and Shane saying nothing. She was grateful for his silence. She couldn't breathe, she couldn't think.

When there were no more tears to cry, Shane stood. A moment later a glass of water appeared before her.

She took a grateful swallow, then heaved a shaky breath.

"Thank you," she whispered.

Shane gestured toward her drawstring flannel pants in muted shades of pink and gray along with a matching, petal-pink Henley. "I see Graham found you some clothes. The color suits you."

"Yeah." She plucked at the fabric stretching over her knee. "From the spa."

He was putting them back on neutral ground again, and for that she was grateful. He wouldn't hold her temporary weakness against her. She'd hold it against herself.

"Hungry?" he asked.

"I suppose."

He took off his coat and they ordered room service from the menu provided. She decided on a fennel and arugula salad with a Pommery emulsion and grilled branzino. Whatever that meant.

Her eyes widened at the price. There was no way she was paying forty-two dollars for a salad with a slab of grilled fish!

Shane brushed away her concerns. "Don't worry. It's on the house."

"Are you sure?"

"Graham owes me. It's a long story."

He didn't elaborate. Come to think of it, he never elaborated when it came to the resort. She didn't know much more about Shane than he knew about her. Whenever the conversation veered into personal territory, he changed the subject or said, "It's a story for another time."

Turned out, another time never came.

She knew his dad had owned the resort before he'd died of a heart attack almost two years ago. The rest she'd picked up from tidbits of gossip she'd tried to avoid but listened to anyway. There was something odd about how his stepbrother had come to own the property. Some said that Shane's dad had cut Shane out of the will entirely. Others said he was left a share in the property that he sold to his stepbrother for one dollar. She didn't believe either story, and she'd never asked Shane for clarification.

The difference between them was that Shane was curious, while she had been content to let sleeping dogs lie.

Now that they were stranded together, she wondered if it might be time to turn the tables on him.

As she pondered Shane's reaction if she were to use his third degree techniques on him, the food arrived on ornate silver platters. The minute the mouthwatering aromas reached her, Kara discovered she was famished.

She recognized the bellhop from town. His name was Colin or Kevin. She discreetly glanced at his name tag: Kevin.

When he discovered the food was for them, Kevin's posture relaxed and a wide grin spread across his boyish face. "Hey, Officer Taylor, Doc. Didn't expect to see you staying here." His face turned a brilliant shade of red. "I mean...you know...since you have a house in town."

There was no way anyone was going to mistake her as coming from the kind of money needed to vacation at the hot springs.

"I know," she said, smiling to ease his embarrassment. "The storm trapped us on the wrong side of the pass."

Kevin rolled his eyes. "They told us. My manager said we'd get a per diem since we have to stay the night. I can use that. My brother and I are buying our ma a washer for Christmas."

Shane glanced up from his phone. "The resort is closed over Christmas, right?"

"Yep." Kevin rubbed his hands together. "Two whole weeks. I like the money, but I could use a break. Since this storm won't let up, the guests are getting grumpy. No clear skies means no viewing the northern lights. They don't tip as well when they're grumpy."

Kara did the mental calculations. Her birthday wasn't that far off.

Kevin chatted about his family while he set up their lunches. "I better get going. The resort manager, Mark, keeps us on a tight watch. He's always checking up on us on the security cameras. Gives me the creeps."

When he'd gone, they ate in companionable silence. Shane had ordered a large T-bone steak with a side of fries. Graham must owe him big, considering what that must have cost.

When they finished, she moved to the love seat once more. He dragged a velvet upholstered barrel chair across the room and set it before her. She knew what was coming. He needed to solve Walt's murder, which meant he needed to know everything that had happened. Though she thought she'd prepared herself, her stomach churned.

His face grave, Shane sank onto the seat and rested his elbows on his bent knees, his hands clasped. "I'm sorry about Walt. I know the two of you were close."

Pressure built again behind her eyes. "Yes."

"We don't have to talk about this now."

Her leg was feeling better and the food had given her a burst of energy.

"No." She vigorously shook her head. "I want to. I want to remember everything while the details are fresh. I don't want to miss anything."

He pulled his phone from his pocket and swiped at the screen. "I'm going to record this, if that's all right. That way, neither of us forgets the details."

"Okay."

He pressed a button, and a red light showed on his phone.

"You worked with Walt in Denali State Park, right?" he asked. "That's how you two met."

"Yes." Her memory flew back across the years. She'd been terrified and woefully inept in the beginning. Thankfully, both the dogs and Walt were patient with her. "We worked with the sled dogs. Walt was the one who encouraged me to apply to vet school."

"I'm glad he did." Shane's expression brightened. "You're a real asset to this community."

Her cheeks heated. "To the animals, you mean."

"Yes. To the animals. But I also mean to the town in general. In a community this small, everyone fills a purpose. You're well-liked and respected around here."

A spark of pride buoyed her spirits. Maybe because she'd moved so much as a kid, she'd never really considered any place she'd lived *home*. While working in Denali, she'd been focused on going to college. Once in college, she'd been focused on getting into vet school. After her graduation, she'd worked at the job Walt helped her get in Anchorage for two years, learning the ropes.

Throughout that time, she'd kept in touch with Walt. He wasn't very good at writing, and he never used email, but he'd call occasionally.

Kara cleared her throat. "He called me about six months ago and said he'd retired and moved back to Kodiak Springs. He said the town needed a good vet."

"I'm glad he called," Shane said. "I didn't know him well, but he sounds like a good man."

"He was. The best."

She'd been alone most of her life, but she'd never been lonely. Not until now.

Shane sobered. "Are you ready to talk about what happened when you arrived at the house?"

The blood rushed in her ears. Using a technique she'd learned in college to control anxiety, she mentally named five things in the room: lamp, chair, table, phone, rug. What had happened was in the past. This was the present.

"I'm ready," she said with a fresh sense of resolve.

She went through the story again, analyzing each moment and grappling to remember even the smallest details. More than once, she slipped out of the present and doubts came at her like battering rams. What if the killer was looking for her and not Walt? What if she'd arrived sooner? What if…what if…what if…?

When the *what ifs* threatened to drown her, she focused on the room again: lamp, chair, table, phone, rug—repeating the mantra until her thoughts calmed.

When she finished, Shane said, "Can you think of any reason someone might want to murder Walt?"

She'd been racking her brain, but she still felt as though all the oxygen had been sucked out of the room. "No. He didn't have an enemy in the world."

Nick Amato was dead. Nick Amato's parents were dead. His son had died of a drug overdose. He didn't have a spouse. He didn't have siblings. From what the marshals had told her, he was unmissed and unmourned. She was being paranoid. After fifteen years looking over her shoulder, she was conditioned for fear.

"Had Walt been acting strangely lately? Any visitors? Anything unusual?"

There was absolutely no reason to go after Walt when she was a much more vulnerable target. It didn't make any sense.

"Nothing," she said. "Walt was as steady as they come. He was all about routine. He ate the same thing every morning. He took care of the dogs. He read in the evenings."

There'd been nothing of note in Walt's or her life these past few weeks. No cars parked down the street. No odd calls. No indication that anyone was looking for her.

"Did Walt have any other relatives? Anyone we need to call?"

"Not that I know of," she said. "He was an only child and he never had any kids. There might be some family in the lower forty-eight, but he'd lost track of them decades ago. Long before I ever knew him." She snapped her fingers. "He mentioned seeing a lawyer in town. But I think it was personal. He'd said he'd known her since they were kids."

They needed to rule out all the possibilities, didn't they? She'd answer his questions first, then tell him about her past. Because once she did, there was no way he'd consider anything in Walt's life as the cause of Walt's murder.

Shane scribbled on a piece of paper. "The attorney is probably Eileen Turro. She's lived here all her life and she's the right age. I'll get in touch with her."

Kara splayed her hands. "Okay."

The air seemed heavier and the room seemed smaller. Nick Amato was dead. There was no one left who cared about a rebellious kid from Florida.

An involuntary shiver raised the hairs on her arms.

Shane stood and reached for a chunky knit blanket draped over the back of the love seat, then extended it to her. "Here."

"Thanks," she mumbled.

He resumed his seat, taking the same stance—elbows on bent knees, hands clasped. Her scalp prickled. From now on, she'd think of that as his "interrogation posture."

"I did some research on Walt." Shane's gaze didn't waver.

Kara shrugged. "Probably wasn't much to find. He lived a quiet life."

Shane was leading her someplace specific. This was

the time to come clean. To tell him first and avoid causing any further suspicion.

"Walt only had two jobs his entire life." Shane forged ahead. "He spent the past twenty years working with the sled dogs at Denali State Park. Tracking down what he did before that was trickier."

Her lungs constricted.

Shane had a slightly regretful air, as though he didn't want to continue, but knew he had to. "Walt was a U.S. Marshal assigned to the Witness Security Program."

Her mouth went dry. She desperately wanted to blurt out the truth, but the words refused to come. She'd kept her secret for so long, she didn't know how to tell the truth anymore.

His voice lowered. "Doesn't take a genius to connect the dots, Kara. You and Walt were always an unlikely pair. Unless, that is, you were placed together for a reason." His pale blue eyes were steady and sincere. "You can trust me. Whatever you say here stays here, but I need to know the truth. For Walt's sake."

She swallowed over the lump in her throat. Once she admitted the truth, there was no going back. She'd have to live with the possibility, however improbable, that she'd caused Walt's death. Though she knew it was irrational, she wanted to put off the possibility, if only for another moment. She'd have to contact the marshals either way. Still, if there'd been a threat, why hadn't they contacted her? They were in the best position to know if she was in danger.

When he realized she wasn't going to reply, Shane asked the question she'd been dreading for more than half her life. "Are you in witness protection?"

SIX

Shane kept his expression carefully neutral as the color drained from Kara's face. Her head dropped to her chest and she clutched the knit blanket more tightly around her shoulders. He wanted to reach out to her. He held himself back.

The most valuable skill in law enforcement was patience.

She swallowed convulsively, her throat working. "Yes. No. Sort of."

One of those answers he'd expected. He wasn't certain what to do with the rest.

His eyebrows drew together. "I don't follow."

"You're right. I've been in the program for almost fifteen years."

"Wait." Shane ran the calculations through his head. "That'd make you...seventeen years old when you went in."

"Eighteen. The age of majority is eighteen in...in where I came from."

He noted her reticence to share her home state. "Who else was placed in the program with you? Parents? Siblings?"

"No one. Just me. That's what I said. Eighteen was the age of majority in Florida."

"Then you haven't spoken to anyone in your family for fifteen years?" he asked, not bothering to hide his incredulity.

Someone even a few months younger would have gone into protection with at least one other family member.

"No."

She said the word with no more emotion than she'd use in a weather report—*sunny skies, no sign of rain.*

Shane closed his eyes for a moment. She was originally from Florida. She'd moved to Alaska fifteen years ago with no family, no friends and no past.

Suddenly weary, he sat back in his chair and swiped a hand over his eyes. He remembered being eighteen. He remembered thinking he knew everything—could conquer anything. He'd been six feet tall and bulletproof. Ready to take on the world. It hadn't taken him long to figure out he had a lot to learn.

Now when he saw eighteen-year-olds, his chest ached at how unbearably *young* they were.

"Walt was your handler?" he asked, struggling to understand how the federal government could think an eighteen-year-old was mature enough to decide their own future.

"Sort of. I wanted to work with animals. One of the guys working my case knew Walt. He put us together."

"Ah."

The pieces instantly fell into place. Walt had been the one constant in the upheaval of her life. He was more than someone she'd worked for at Denali State Park. Knowing Walt had been with her since the beginning of her time in the program explained her fierce protectiveness of him. It also explained her unwillingness to hear any criticism of him.

He was the closest thing she had to family.

All the questions he'd wanted to ask seemed meaningless now. What did that sort of separation do to a person? To be ripped from everything you knew and everyone you loved. She'd been little more than a kid. Yet somehow she'd survived. Even thrived. Vet school was harder to get into than medical school. He'd always known Kara was special, but he had a new admiration for her tenacious spirit.

Shane straightened. Despite his personal feelings, he had a job to do. They both wanted to find Walt's killer.

"You wavered before," he said. "Initially you stated you were in the program, then you said you weren't. Which is it?"

"The guy I gave evidence on died earlier this year," she said, her voice barely more than a whisper. "He was the only person who was a danger to me. The threat level was deemed low once he died. Low enough that if I decided to voluntarily leave the program, I doubt they'd put up much of a fuss."

"Are you certain of that?" he asked.

"I can't be certain of anything, but I don't understand how this could be connected." This time her voice held a note of conviction. "Maybe someone wanted revenge in the beginning, but fifteen years in civilian life is like fifty years in street life. People die. Leadership changes. People go straight. I doubt anyone even remembers Nick, let alone mourns him."

A fresh wave of sympathy enveloped Shane. Kara was tough, it was one of the things he admired about her.

Now he wondered how much she had suffered to earn her thick skin.

"The guy you put in jail must have been dangerous," Shane said. "They wouldn't have entered you in the program otherwise."

She snorted a humorless laugh. "He was dangerous, yes. And he wasn't too happy with me, that's for sure. He put a hit on me during the trial, then tried a couple times from jail. The marshals kept an eye on him. After a few years, he stopped trying. Didn't seem like he cared anymore."

Shane absorbed her matter-of-fact words. At some level, she'd spent the past fifteen years in fear. Always looking over her shoulder. Always wondering if the passing stare of a stranger revealed a threat. Always waiting for a phone call giving her bad news. Had she ever felt safe?

He caught her expectant gaze and started from his reverie. "Did you witness a murder?"

What else would put an eighteen-year-old in the program?

"Yes," she said, straightening her spine.

"Do you want to tell me what happened?"

"The details don't matter. I witnessed a murder, and my testimony put the guy in jail."

"I'll need a name, at least. To look up the case."

"Nick Amato. It was a big story at the time and all over the news. They kept my name out of the papers, but there's plenty of references to an unidentified witness."

The name Nick Amato rang a bell, but Shane didn't remember the details. He'd look it up later.

"And your contact in the marshals?"

"Tom Winter."

She rattled off his number.

Shane wasn't surprised she didn't want to relive the event, and he didn't press her. Sometimes people wanted to talk, as though telling the story from a distance excised the memories. Some people simply wanted to bottle it up and pretend nothing ever happened.

He tipped his head back and studied the ceiling with a thousand-yard stare. Her answers left a lot of holes to be filled. Ninety-nine percent of the people in WITSEC were criminals. Unlike in the movies, the average joe rarely witnessed a crime. People on the wrong side of the law were generally the ones hanging out in the dark alley when the bullets started flying.

"I know what you're thinking," she said, her voice growing stronger. "But I wasn't involved. I was in the wrong place at the wrong time. That's all."

He lowered his gaze. "You don't know what I was thinking."

"Then what were you?" she demanded, her posture defensive.

"I was thinking how incredibly young you must have been." He rarely spoke of his own past. Certainly not when he was acting in a professional capacity. He decided to make an exception. Just this once. "After my mom died, I spent a lot of time with an aunt who lives in Anchorage. When I turned eighteen, she pulled me aside and said something that I never forgot. She said, *You can leave everything behind you now. Any regrets. Any shame. Any mistakes you made. You can let it all go and start fresh. Kids do dumb stuff because they're kids. Don't spend the rest of your life beating yourself up over it.*"

He hadn't understood what she was trying to tell him

until years later. "She knew that I had regrets about my mom's death. Things I should have said. Things I should have done. She gave me permission to let go of that weight. She was right. We do the best we can with what we have. We can't expect kids to make adult decisions and then punish them for making immature choices."

Her eyes reddened and the tip of her nose turned pink.

He sighed inwardly. The thought that her past might have had something to do with Walt's death was crushing her. The fact that she'd been living with the threat from Nick Amato for fifteen years must have done a number on her, as well. It was no wonder she wasn't interested in giving out a lot of personal details. For the past fifteen years, one slipup risked her life.

What an insensitive jerk he'd been while they were dating. He'd assumed there was something wrong with *him*. He'd been defensive rather than understanding.

Uncertain of his current standing with her, he stood and crossed the distance between them, then sat on the edge of the sofa beside her. He fixed his gaze straight ahead.

"Thank you," he said. "For telling me. There's a lot of ways this can go. The work Walt did for the marshals was dangerous. Who's to say that someone didn't wait twenty years to get revenge on him? Nothing is certain, and I can't rule out anything."

Walt's murder didn't fit with a professional hit aimed at Kara. The collateral damage was unnecessary. If someone had come this far to kill her, she was an easy target. She lived alone. She traveled alone. She worked with the public.

He also had to consider the information the marshals had. They didn't lower the threat level for people from the program unless they knew for certain the danger was mitigated.

She tipped into him, resting her cheek against his shoulder. He turned and wrapped both arms around her, holding her close, wishing there was something he could do to make her pain disappear. Even for a moment.

Her closest friend, someone who'd been a father to her, had been murdered. And there was a chance someone from her past was the most likely suspect.

Until he learned differently, all possibilities were on the table. He'd done an initial search of the hotel's guest list and come up empty. The resort had fifty guests and all of them had traveled with a spouse or companion, which made twenty-five pairs. Only a handful of them were under sixty, and nothing in any of their backgrounds had raised an alarm.

An initial search of the employees had come up empty, as well. Including Graham, there were fifteen employees on site. Thus far, all of their alibis checked out. It appeared the killer had taken a different escape route. But even though everything looked clear at the resort, he was keeping his guard up.

He had too many questions and no answers in sight. For now, all he could give her was comfort.

Kara's hair was silky against his fingers. The same thought he'd had for weeks whispered through his head. He wanted to know whether there could be something between them again. Even if it was only friendship. Maybe if he did things right this time, instead of getting caught up in his own insecurities, they could get along.

She trusted him a little just now. Enough to share her painful truth. There was a glimmer of hope that in time that trust might grow. He missed her. He missed talking with her, laughing with her, debating with her. Their last argument had been stupid and unnecessary. He'd gladly lose all the arguments if they could go back to being friends.

She didn't need any of that burden right now. What she needed was someone to understand the depth of her loss. That much he could do.

As they sat like that, neither talking, their thoughts drifting to things long since forgotten, the floor trembled.

For a moment the odd sensation didn't register, then it hit him. Adrenaline spiked through his system.

He sprang to his feet and started toward the window.

The crystal chandelier overhead jingled merrily. A low rumble rattled the windowpanes. He'd been fearing this for so long, it seemed almost inevitable now.

Kara raised her startled gaze to him. "What is it? Is that an earthquake?"

He'd felt something similar once before, and he'd never forgotten the sensation. "It's an avalanche. And it's a big one."

The lobby was in pandemonium.

Kara leaned against a narrow table at the back of the room, away from the melee. Her leg ached and her head pounded with the noise. The cheerful Christmas lights strung from the rafters were at odds with the mood of the crowd. What had started as a light grumbling had turned into a cacophony of voices demanding answers.

Graham was attempting to bring order to the confusion. The differences between the stepbrothers were striking. While Shane appeared as though he belonged outdoors, Graham was strictly corporate. His jeans had a little too much bling, and his Western shirt with its mother-of-pearl snaps probably cost more than Kara's entire wardrobe. His blond hair and gym-sculpted build reminded her of the jock character from an eighties movie aimed at teenagers.

While Shane seemed to be a product of his rugged surroundings, Graham struck her as being purposefully manufactured. Like he was trying too hard to look like he wasn't trying at all.

He raised his arms and flashed his palms. "There's no need to be alarmed. We're assessing the situation. I'll have answers for you as soon as possible."

The din of incensed voices never faltered. Shane and another man had left over an hour ago to assess the damage. The more time that went by without news, the more anxious the guests were becoming.

Cell phone reception was spotty, and the landlines had been knocked out by the avalanche. That's all anyone knew for certain.

Graham's reassurance was doing nothing to quiet the growing dissent in the crowded lobby. She searched the flood of guests and her attention landed on a man separate from the crowd.

He stood in a small alcove, his stance rigid and his arms crossed stiffly. His gaze was intense, and it didn't waver when he noticed her interest. He was staring at her.

Goosebumps prickled along her arms.

His large, square tortoiseshell glasses dominated his face. Amber-tinted lenses prevented her from seeing his eyes.

"Please," Graham called, drawing her attention to the front of the room once more. "Let's retire to the dining room for coffee and drinks while we sort this all out."

When she glanced back at the man in the alcove, his interest had focused elsewhere.

She turned to the older woman beside her and gestured. "Do you know who that is?"

The woman shrugged. "I don't know. He's an odd duck, that's for sure. Doesn't spend much time with the guests. He's always down by the hot springs."

"I said," Graham shouted over the disgruntled chatter. "Dessert is available in the dining room."

Judging by the noise level, no one was interested in dessert.

The man in the glasses flashed a look of disgust toward Graham, glanced at her, then swiveled on his heel. Kara's heart raced. She wasn't paranoid. He'd been watching her.

She started to follow him, but the front door swung open.

Shane tromped through it. His pants were covered in snow up to his thighs, his hat was coated and his beard was white with flakes.

A low murmur rippled through the crowd. Heads turned. Voices grew hushed. Annoyance tripped across Graham's face, but it was quickly followed by relief when he realized Shane's presence had quieted the crowd.

Graham had been trying to bring order for the past hour, and Shane had calmed the crowd without a word. He joined Graham at the front of the room.

Shane scraped his hat from his head and ran his fingers through his dark hair, mussing the strands. Her fingers itched to smooth it before her gaze dropped to his lips. She'd never kissed him with a beard.

She jerked upright. Where had that thought come from?

"Okay, folks," he began, "I'll give you the good news first. Because of the quick action of the local troopers, there are no injuries to report." A wave of relieved murmurs undulated through the crowd. "Now for the bad news. The road is completely impassable."

The room exploded into nervous chatter.

A woman in an ivory fisherman's sweater held up her hand like an eager schoolchild. "What does that mean for us?"

Shane turned his head and spoke softly to Graham. They exchanged a few more sentences before he faced the crowd once more.

"I've been informed there are more than enough supplies for a day or two. Helicopters are grounded until further notice." Graham whispered something and Shane nodded. "The Wi-Fi is working fine and the kitchen has prepared a dessert buffet in the dining room for anyone who's interested. The home page on the television in your room will have the latest updates."

Shoulders sagged and voices calmed. An elderly gentleman with a salt-and-pepper beard turned toward the dining area. The others in the lobby, as though released from some sort of stupor, turned to follow.

Shane strode toward Kara. The milling guests, perhaps sensing his purpose, parted.

He stopped and she tilted back her head, looking up and up and up into his scowling face.

"You shouldn't be putting weight on that leg," he said. "Doctor's orders."

"I'm fine," she replied, her eyebrows raised. "And I was as curious as everyone else about the avalanche."

"You shouldn't be out of your room. Not without me or one of the security guards."

"We've been over this. No one staying at the hotel

fits the description of a killer. Besides, no one is going to murder me in a crowd of people."

"You don't know that."

"You win. I will no longer appear in public without an armed guard."

"Good." He glanced over his shoulder, then guided her farther away from any curious ears. "We can't afford to make a mistake. Clearing the road in two to three days is optimistic. Which means we're all trapped here." With another glance over his shoulder, he continued, "Let's get you back to your room. There's something we need to talk about."

The tone of his voice set off alarm bells.

His phone buzzed.

He glanced at the number and heaved a sigh. "It'll have to wait another ten minutes. Can you wait for me in the dining room?"

"Aren't you worried I'll be murdered over the cheesecake?"

"I may have overreacted. Slightly. Grab me a piece of chocolate cake."

Kara made her way to the vaulted dining room and studied the crowd. About twenty or so people had decided to take advantage of Graham's offer.

She limped to a table near the enormous double doors. Noting her injury, a waiter offered to serve her.

As she ordered, she caught sight of the man who'd been staring at her in the lobby. He was making his way to the buffet.

Kara slouched, putting the waiter between herself and the man's view. Confident he hadn't seen her, she followed his progress to one of the empty tables.

This had to be the safest place in the hotel right now.

There were cameras mounted in the corners, and plenty of people around. Shane's initial searches had come up empty on the guests.

Gathering her courage, she stood. She wouldn't have to worry about a murder after this because Shane was going to kill her.

SEVEN

Kara took a seat next to the man and stuck out her hand. "I'm Kara Riley. I just checked in. How about that avalanche?"

On the off chance he was here to kill her, there was no point in hiding her identity. He'd already know who she was.

He was shorter than average with a higher BMI than he probably wanted. His beard beneath the tortoiseshell glasses was scruffy in that artful way men groomed themselves in order to look like they just rolled out of bed. His cinnamon-brown cable-knit sweater featured a patch on one shoulder and blended seamlessly with the color of his hair and eyes. She could picture him wearing a bush hat with one of the sides pinned up.

His fork hovered in the air. "Oh, um, nice to meet you."

She let her hand drop. "How's the cake?"

"Good." His gaze skittered away, then back to her. "Everything is good here."

Her nerves prickled. He seemed out of place among the guests. Everyone else in the room reeked of entitlement. This guy looked like he was afraid someone was going to snatch his dessert if he let down his guard.

"Have you stayed here before?" she asked.

"First time."

His voice didn't set off any alarm bells, but she'd only heard Walt's killer's voice raised in anger. Not exactly a situation she wanted to re-create in a crowded dining room.

Using his index finger, he pushed his glasses up the bridge of his nose. "I'm Finn Dyer, by the way. I'm a—a geologist. I've been studying the hot springs." He shifted in his seat. "It's fascinating work. Quite a few organisms can survive and even thrive in the heated water." A flush crept up his neck. "I'm boring you."

That definitely did not sound like the opening salvo of a cold-blooded killer. Then again, maybe pretending to be a bashful geologist was part of his cover. Or maybe she'd watched too many police procedurals over the years. She was applying artificial menace to even the most mundane situations.

"No, no," she protested. "I'm all ears."

"You're the veterinarian, aren't you?"

That got her attention. "Yes."

"I saw you in the lobby and figured it was you. You're just like Walt said."

"W-wait," she stuttered. "You talked to Walt?"

He flushed. "Yeah. Once."

"We were…we're close." She swiftly corrected herself. "What did you talk about?"

He lifted one shoulder in careless indifference. "Nothing. Just stuff."

"Like what kind of stuff?"

"He talked about his dogs a lot. He liked history. He knew everything about the Indigenous tribes in the area."

"You said he mentioned me?" she prodded, raising her voice at the end for encouragement.

Finn wasn't much of a talker. This was worse than pulling teeth.

"Oh, yeah. He asked if I'd met you yet. Said you sometimes came by the resort to check on the sled dogs. Said you were good with animals. Say, um, he was supposed to get back to me on something. If you talk to him, can you remind him to call me?"

Either he was a very good actor, or he was legitimately unaware that Walt had been murdered.

"Sure," she said. "Can I leave him a message?"

"Nah. He had a book on the Tlingit Native Alaskans. Did you know they used the hot springs for sweat bathing? They thought it treated arthritis, colds and even stress. Go figure. I guess stress isn't just a modern invention." He fanned his fingers. "The springs were said to enhance overall well-being."

"People must still believe they do." She waved one hand to encompass the room. "The resort does a good business."

Finn's expression darkened. "There's nothing people and money won't exploit. It's sad if you think about it. A culture survives for thousands of years, and then, one day, someone comes along and says, 'Never mind. This all belongs to me.'"

She wanted to keep him talking. "Sometimes progress is just exchanging one problem for another."

"You know that quote by Honoré de Balzac?"

"I'm not sure I do."

"*Behind every great fortune lies a great crime.* Makes me think of that. Only behind every great exploration is a great tragedy." Finn glanced toward the corner of the room where a security camera was suspended from the ceiling. "Do you trust that state trooper?"

She followed his gaze. "Officer Taylor, you mean?"

He seemed to be distracted by the cameras, yet he was making no effort to move out of view.

"Yes," Finn said, focusing his attention on her once more. "I saw you talking just now. I figured you must know him."

"I do. He's a good man. He's a good officer. You can trust him." The waiter discovered her new seat and set down the two pieces of cake and two decaf coffees. "If you want to talk to him, he's going to join me when he finishes his phone call."

She pointed at the two place settings to make her point.

"Never mind," Finn said. "It's nothing."

"I can give him a message if you want."

"That's all right." Finn adjusted his glasses again. "Can you do me a favor? Don't tell anyone I was asking about the cop."

The only time in her life she hadn't wanted people to see her speaking to the police was when she was hanging out with people who were operating on the wrong side of the law. Finn didn't look like the type, but she wasn't taking any chances.

"They sure have a lot of cameras here, don't they?" she said. "Makes you feel safe."

"Makes me feel like big brother is watching." Finn snorted. "Since I'm not a paying guest like the others, I feel like the management is always watching to make sure I don't steal the silver."

She'd had people look down their noses at her plenty of times. She knew the feeling. "These places can be intimidating, can't they?"

"That's putting it mildly."

He pushed his plate toward the center of the table and swiveled in his seat. She didn't have much time.

She flagged down a waiter and grabbed a pen, then scribbled Shane's number on a napkin. "You can call Sergeant Taylor." She added her own number. "Or me. Anytime. If you need anything."

He scooted his chair back and her stomach sank. His demeanor changed from defensive to indifferent in the blink of an eye. Whatever had been bothering him before clearly didn't matter anymore.

"Don't worry about it." Finn stuffed the number in his pocket and stood. "I had a legal question, is all."

He walked to the door and she'd almost convinced herself that he was a dead end. There was nothing to connect him to Walt except a fascination with history and a fear of *damnatio memoriae*. He and Walt wanted to preserve history against the powers of colonial guilt that made it easier to erase the past than admit mistakes.

At least he'd taken the phone number. Maybe he'd change his mind. At the very least, he'd spoken with Walt recently. If there was any chance he'd seen or heard something, they had to know.

As Finn exited the dining room, he glanced up at the camera suspended above him, then back at her. An emotion radiated from him like a heat wave, though she couldn't quite gauge the meaning.

Was it fear? Was it guilt? He turned away before she could identify the source of his unease.

"I'll talk with the geologist, Kara," Shane repeated for the third time. "It's only been a few hours."

He'd sought Kara out as soon as he was able. He was

running on fumes. He hadn't slept much last night and wasn't anticipating doing any better tonight. This day had started out bad and gotten worse. He was ready to hang it up and start again tomorrow.

He'd coordinated the road clearing with Jeff as soon as the weather let up, contacted the marshal from WIT-SEC and stressed the continued danger to Kara with the resort security. The storm hadn't abated long enough to bring in the helicopter, and Shane was on edge.

Since the avalanche had occurred closer to the resort, Major Crimes was scheduled to retrieve Walt's body for an autopsy to learn more about the gun that had killed him as soon as weather permitted. Which left Shane trapped and ineffective while the case progressed without him. Each additional minute that ticked past grated on his nerves. The nagging voice in his head reminded him that the Alaska Bureau of Investigations was better equipped and had more technical capabilities. They were trained to study murder scenes.

A different, louder voice was trying to drown out his better sense. This was his case and his borough, and somewhere along the line things had gotten personal.

In between everything else, he'd been attempting to track down the geologist, Finn. He'd even had resort security on the lookout. It was a small resort, yet Finn always managed to be someplace else when Shane wanted to talk with him.

"Finn was one of the last people to speak with Walt," Kara said. "And he was nervous about something. I don't know how it all fits together, but I can't shake the feeling it's something important."

"I believe you, but I'm spread thin. If he wants to avoid me, he's doing a good job."

Shane only had two eyes and that wasn't enough lately. He needed to be everywhere at once and he was winding up nowhere.

"Can't you go to his room or something?" she asked.

"I tried his room already," Shane said. "I'm telling you, I've dealt with reluctant people before. If he doesn't want anyone to know he's talking to me, then hanging around outside his door will only frighten him worse."

Shane was balancing on a fine line. He wanted to speak with Finn as much as Kara did. If he couldn't find the geologist soon, he was certain Kara would take matters into her own hands. That was something he wanted to avoid at all costs. He didn't even like the idea of her talking to Finn in the dining room surrounded by people and staff. Not until he knew more.

"I know, I know." She pressed her fisted hands against her temples. "You're right. I'm just frustrated."

He needed her to understand he was taking this seriously. "If you think Finn murdered Walt, if you recognize his voice, then I can act in my capacity as a state trooper to detain him. Beyond that, I can only request a conversation. I can't force him."

"No." Her posture sagged as though someone had clipped the strings holding her erect. "He didn't strike me as a murderer and his voice wasn't familiar. One of the other guests said he was always kinda twitchy. It seems to be his default state."

"One good thing came out of your talk already," Shane said. "Because he wasn't a paying guest or an official employee, he wasn't listed on the manifest, which means Jeff and I hadn't done a preliminary background check on him. He works for the University of Anchorage. Looks like he's been there for at least a decade. Nothing suspicious there. All we know is that he visited Walt, and he asked if I was trustworthy. We don't even know the two things are connected."

"Nothing about this makes any sense. If this is about Nick Amato, how does a geologist from Anchorage trace back to me?"

"I'll try and find him as soon as I leave here. He can't go anywhere. None of us can."

"I should have pushed him harder to tell me why he visited Walt." Kara rubbed the heels of her hands against her eyes. "Being trapped here is making me frustrated. I can't stop my mind from spinning and spinning around all the questions."

"I know. Me too."

"I want to know. I have to know. But finding out this is all my fault isn't going to make anything better."

"Let up on yourself." Shane took her fisted hand and she unfurled her fingers. He rubbed his thumb against her palm. "We're doing everything we can. The ABI is doing a deeper search of the guest list and the travel manifests for any inconsistencies. I've recruited two of the security guards from the hotel to check security footage and pinch-hit for me guarding your room. Until I get backup, that's the best I can do."

"I didn't mean to criticize your work," she said, clasping his hand between hers. He wanted to capture this moment. He wanted to memorize the way her fingers felt against his palm and the way her smile wrapped him in comfort like a warm blanket. "I know you're running yourself ragged and I appreciate that. I never doubt your dedication to the job. I admire you for it."

"You have a strange way of showing it," he mumbled, sliding his hand free of her grasp. "You don't like this uniform. You don't like my job. You don't like how I'm handling this case. Is there anything you like about me?"

She lifted her stricken gaze to him. "I like everything about you. Don't you realize that?"

"If that were true, we'd be together. We're not."

"Liking each other was never the problem with us."

"Then what is the problem? If we can't even be friends, then what you're saying is a lie."

Her eyes glazed over, and she went unnaturally still. "You don't understand."

His injured speech burned in his throat, refusing to cooperate. "Then explain it to me."

"I can't."

He'd known from the beginning he was more invested in the relationship than Kara was. There was no reason to feel hurt. "Then there's nothing left to say."

Her voice was small and distant. "I'm sorry."

The last thing he needed was her pity. Maybe being friends wasn't such a good idea after all. Maybe it was time to cut his losses.

"I'm sorry too," he said with a sigh.

She looked sad and he froze the image of her then. He never let anyone else have power over him. There were no unfinished relationships in his past. No unrequited loves boxed away in the recesses of his memory. He'd always been good at floating above the drama of romance that had sucked so many of his friends beneath the surface.

Love was a weapon of manipulation that he refused to let someone use against him. Loving someone meant giving them power. The more uneven the relationship, the more uneven the power structure.

If he stayed in control, he'd insulate himself from a broken heart. That's why he'd walked away from their relationship without hesitation. He stood by his decision. Why, then, did it bother him that he felt as though he'd been unceremoniously dumped like a pair of shoes that pinched? And why did he care so much?

Her gaze grew wistful. "What are you thinking?"

He stood. "I'm thinking it's time to get back to work."

She went to push off from the couch and winced. "I may have overdone it today."

"Let me help."

He extended his arm, and she slipped her palm into his hand, allowing him to haul her upright.

She was even lighter than he remembered, and he inadvertently propelled her into his chest. She flattened her palm against his beating heart to steady herself. He bent his head and his good intentions fled. Her eyes reminded him of warm butterscotch.

He swallowed hard against the rush of unfamiliar emotions crowding him. Close proximity to Kara was not conducive to his peace of mind. One glance from her left him rattled. For a moment her expression seemed almost wistful. Had she enjoyed any of their time together? Did she ever regret what happened between them?

The argument had been stupid. A disagreement that should have been laughed off. Instead, they'd both become stubbornly entrenched.

He'd felt compelled to stand his ground. She'd scared him because he sensed that he would always love her more. He'd been scared of the shift in power, scared of letting her have control over him. He was right to be afraid.

His gaze dropped to her lips and for a moment he was tempted. He stood there, captivated and speechless. More enticed than he ever recalled being in his life. They were both drowning in emotion, but this time, Kara was the more vulnerable of the two.

The realization rose like a wall between them. She was no more ready to deal with the uncertainty of their relationship than he was.

He lifted his hands to her shoulders and pressed a kiss to her forehead, letting his lips linger a touch longer than a friendly peck, then he stepped away.

They stood there like that for a long moment, neither of them speaking. He gave Kara every opportunity to reach out to him.

She plastered a fake smile on her face, presumably to camouflage the awkward moment. "At least we'll be out of here by Christmas."

He let his heart adjust to the disappointment.

Things were going to be harder from here on out. "I hope so. I'm already sick of wearing this uniform."

He didn't enjoy holidays in general, and Christmas in particular. As a trooper, he saw that most holidays were excuses for bad behavior. Christmas was just another chance for people to assume fake smiles in front of a fake tree and appear fake happy.

"I love Christmas." A thoughtful smile touched her lips, as though she'd wrapped her mind around a pleasant memory. "No one ever forgets to celebrate, do they?"

"I guess not." Something tugged at the edges of his memory, a fact that was just beyond his reach.

He made a mental note of her enthusiasm. He couldn't recall a time he'd seen her this excited. She didn't strike him as the sort who'd festoon her house with Christmas decorations. He tried to picture her spare front room filled with a porcelain village set on spun glass snow, an electric train circling the base of a fresh-cut pine and yards of twinkling colored lights. No matter how hard he tried, he couldn't. But what did he know about her? Not much, apparently.

Come to think of it, it wouldn't take much to slip into the gift shop and see if he could find a present. The few high-end items the resort carried were probably nicer than anything he'd find in town. While he and Kara weren't in the sort of relationship that meant they exchanged presents, he didn't think she'd have much under the tree. Not considering her past, and especially now that Walt was gone. This was how it was going to be between them.

The differences between them were too vast.

"If you need anything," he said. "I'm in the room next door."

She nodded, her attention fixed on the blowing snow outside the window.

That nagging sensation returned. As though he was forgetting something. He mentally shrugged. He'd figure it out later. Right now he was tired, and he couldn't afford to be tired. There were too many people counting on him.

A soft tap on the door was followed by, "Resort manager."

Shane swung it open and he recognized Mark. Graham had recruited him from Boston or New York. The resort manager always had the look of a man who wished he was someplace else. He also insisted the staff call him *sir*.

Working in Alaska in the winter meant you were either a native or something had gone terribly wrong in your life. Shane had initially pegged Mark for the latter. When his preliminary background check didn't turn up anything, Shane considered another possibility. Mark was using his job here as a stepping-stone to something bigger. There was no fault in a guy who wanted to move up the ladder.

It was a good reminder to avoid leaping to conclusions.

Shane swung the door open wider. "Can I help you?"

Mark adjusted the perfect double Windsor knot at his neck and flashed an envelope. "Someone left this for Dr. Riley in the lobby."

"Who?"

"I can't say. It was discovered at the check-in desk."

Shane studied the envelope. Kara's first and last names were printed neatly on the outside. She didn't know anyone at the hotel. Whatever was in that envelope was suspect.

"Can you check the security cameras?" he asked. "See if you can find who left this?"

"Certainly. I'll let you know if I discover anything."

Shane took the envelope and shut the door as Mark turned away.

Kara was at his side in an instant. "What is it?"

He peeled open the flap. "Let's find out."

Inside was a postcard. The back was blank save for the words To, From and Postage Here. There was no stamp. No address.

He flipped over the card and Kara gasped.

The front was a gaudy hue of yellow with large block letters containing a different picture in the body of each. There were orange trees and palm leaves and a sunny beach scene. It was the sort of postcard a harried traveler picked up at the airport.

The text read: *Greetings from Florida.*

Below that, someone had scrawled a message in red sharpie: *An eye for an eye is never enough.*

EIGHT

Kara sucked in a ragged breath. "I don't understand."

His face grim, Shane carefully set the postcard on the narrow table beside the door. "This was planned. It had to be. It's not like you can buy a postcard from Florida in the gift shop."

"I don't get it." She held up her hands as though warding off the truth. "I don't get any of this. How did some-one find me? My records are sealed. Why come after me now? Now that Nick is dead? What's the point?"

Not once had she ever contacted anyone from her old life. She'd been using the same identity for so long, she barely remembered who she'd been before. How did someone else?

"I don't know," Shane said. "This feels off."

A scorching wave of anger singed her. "I'm contacting the marshals immediately." She spoke through clenched teeth. "If someone leaked my identity or my location, then the information came from the marshals' office."

She was furious at the marshals but more furious at herself. A part of her had known all along she was re-sponsible for Walt's death. She simply hadn't wanted to face the truth. If she held on to the anger, she could forestall the grief and shame for another few hours. Anything to alleviate the pain. The guilt was rolling across her like a slow-moving glacier, grinding everything in its path to dust.

"Sit," Shane ordered gently. "Let's think about this before we jump to any conclusions."

"How can we *not* jump to conclusions?" She threw up her hands. "It's obvious, isn't it?"

Only two days ago everything had been normal. Right. Then the bottom had dropped out of her world. She felt as if she might shatter at any moment. She perched on the edge of the sofa and hung her head, praying she'd wake from the nightmare.

A gentle hand touched her chin, and Shane urged her to meet his gaze. His touch was soothing, his understanding reached through her, warming her. She'd always thought being alone was the better choice. There was safety in solitude. At least that's what she'd thought. A chill swept through her. Having someone share her burden was a luxury she didn't deserve.

"No matter what happens," he said, "Walt's death was not your fault."

"But—"

"No buts. You are not responsible for someone else's action."

Her gut knotted. When she'd heard Nick Amato had died, she'd taken her first full breath in fifteen years. She'd let herself relax her guard. Kodiak Springs was another fresh start and a new beginning. She was going to put down roots this time. She was finally going to have a *home*.

"Why didn't he kill me?" she asked in a watery voice. "Why did it have to be Walt?"

This end was inevitable. Every good thing in her life had gone bad, one way or another. It was only a matter of time before this interlude of happiness ended. Every time she found her footing, it seemed like something came along and knocked her back down.

"I don't know why Walt was killed," Shane said. "All I know is that something about this doesn't feel right.

"Walt was killed because he knew me. That's why. I'm the only connection. This proves it."

"But why the cloak-and-dagger with the postcard? Why not simply finish the job?"

"To let me know I'm next."

"To what purpose, though? The more bread crumbs he leaves behind, the more he risks getting caught. This feels personal. Immediate. Who in Nick's life held that kind of a grudge for fifteen years?"

"What if he's not dead?" She recognized she was grasping wildly at straws, but she didn't care. "What if Nick, I don't know, faked his death and now he's after me?"

Shane hoisted an eyebrow. "If he was smart enough to fool a prison guard, a medical examiner and an embalmer, he's not going to be dumb enough to trap himself in Alaska at an isolated resort. He'd need plastic surgery, as well. I studied the case. I saw his picture. You could spot that nose from across a football field."

His doubt gave her pause. She touched the spot on her forehead where he'd kissed her. For a moment when he held her, she'd thought she saw hurt in his eyes. That didn't make sense. When they'd argued, he hadn't seemed the least bit fazed by walking away from her. He'd always been independent and self-contained, so the idea that something she said could hurt him rocked her back a step.

How had everything in her life gotten so off balance? No one was behaving the way she expected them to, least of all Shane.

"Wait a second." She narrowed her gaze. "I don't get it. This morning you were certain this was about me. Now we have proof and you're waffling."

Why the sudden change in Shane's opinion?

He threaded his hands behind his head, then lowered his arms to his sides once more. "All I can do is trust my gut. Someone is making a concerted effort to let us know your cover has been blown."

"He wants to see me suffer before he kills me."

"Except he already tried to kill you." Shane gestured toward her leg. "You've got the bullet wound to prove it."

They were both frustrated. Kara felt as though someone had mixed up the pieces of two different puzzles and put them in the same box. They were finding patches of evidence that fit together but also appeared to be totally separate.

There was only one way to make certain they hadn't missed anything. She had to put *all* the pieces on the table.

She pushed aside the sorrow that threatened to overwhelm her.

"If this all leads back to Nick Amato," she said. "Then I need to tell you everything. Not just what you can read in a report or in the papers. All of it." Well, almost all of it. There were some details that she'd never surrender. Not to anyone. "I want to talk about my case. The one that put me in WITSEC."

His expression softened. "Even if we discover the *why*, I'm not sure that's going to help us find the *who*. The killer could be anyone at this point."

"I want to do this." What was the point of hiding anymore? She'd already lost the person who mattered most in her life. "I should have told you everything. If something from my past is the key to solving Walt's murder, we have to consider every detail. No matter how small."

He was wavering. She watched the play of emotions across his face until Sergeant Capital T Taylor prevailed. The officer in him knew she was right— the postcard had forced her hand.

"Okay," he said with a decided lack of enthusiasm. "We can talk. I've read the newspaper reports already. The minute this gets to be too much, we stop. Agreed?"

Immediately after the murder, she hadn't been able to go a day without seeing Jack's face. Now weeks went past without the memory surfacing. She feared that if she spoke about what happened that day, Jack would be with her again. In the present.

In her nightmares.

"Agreed."

Shane moved to the seat across from her. He pulled out his phone and swiped at the screen, then set it on the low coffee table between them. She had an unsettling echo of déjà vu.

Shane pressed a button to start the recording. "Do you give your permission for me to record this?" he asked.

"I do."

Another time, she might have laughed at the odd turn of phrase.

"Tell me about that day."

Her appearance in court had been the last time she'd spoken about the case. There'd been no reason to relive that awful day. Attached to the horror and grief was an underlying sense of guilt that she hadn't completely understood. Not until now.

Kara sucked in a fortifying breath. "We moved around a lot growing up. Me and my mom. Sometimes she'd have a boyfriend, sometimes she didn't." Seeing the question on Shane's face, shame scorched through her. "I never knew my real dad. I don't even think my mom was certain who he was. When we moved to Jacksonville, Florida, things were mostly the same. Then mom started dating Jack. He repossessed cars for a living. He was good at it. He taught me all the tricks of the trade."

"Like how to get a car in neutral if you don't have the key?"

"Yep. He was the only one of mom's boyfriends that was halfway normal. Didn't take her long to break up with him. She never liked the nice guys." The wind had picked up again, and Kara stared at her reflection in the window. "When I turned eighteen, I went to work for Jack. Mostly clerical stuff." Her stomach knotted. "He repossessed the wrong car one day. Seemed like a regular job. Turned out the car belonged to Nick Amato's son, and there was something in the car Nick wanted back."

The harder she fought against the emotions attached to the memories, the deeper they pulled her down. Most times when memories from her past surfaced, they felt disconnected, as though she was looking at another person. In an instant, however, everything abruptly became real and immediate.

"So Nick came looking for the car," Shane prodded, startling her from her reverie. "What happened then?"

She felt herself slipping into the past and feared if she slipped too far, she'd be stuck in a dead-end life again. Forever this time.

"I'd gone outside to smoke a cigarette." The nicotine helped alleviate the worry. She'd been arrested for felony shoplifting, and the idea of doing time was weighing heavy on her mind. "They used to keep a Dumpster out back behind a wooden fence. One day the Dumpster just disappeared. I guess someone stopped paying the bill. Didn't bother us any. We set up a table and a couple of chairs in the spot. It was our unofficial breakroom."

The air was hot and thick and smelled like putrid garbage and overflowing ashtrays. As though the stench of the missing Dumpster was permanently embedded in the asphalt. The bell over the front door rang, and she heard it open and shut. Instead of stubbing out her cigarette, she took another long drag. Let Jack handle this one. She had other things on her mind.

The public defender had called her that morning with a plea deal. Six months in lockup, one year probation. She was considering the offer. She'd done some time in juvie and knew what to expect. Copping a felony had her worried, though. When she was a kid, she couldn't wait to be an adult. No more social workers. No more living with her mom. No more fending off her mom's latest boyfriend. Now, barely four months past her eighteenth birthday, she'd botched it good. Every job application asked the same question: Have you ever been convicted of a felony?

She'd be permanently marked and stuck in a revolving door of dead-end jobs for the rest of her life. She couldn't work for Jack forever. He was already talking about getting out of the business.

The sound of breaking glass startled her from the sagging bands of plastic that passed for a seat on her rusted chair. Some instinct told her to stay hidden behind the privacy fence.

Jack stumbled backward out the door, his hands raised. She followed his progress through the narrow slats of the fence. Two men stalked his escape. One of them was tall and beefy with flat, lifeless eyes. The other was stockier and short, his hair thinning. He wore khakis and a button-up shirt. He might have been a retiree in a bowling league if not for the gun in his right hand.

Her scream died in her throat and she stood frozen.

Jack stuck out his arm, his palm toward her. He was signaling to her to stay put.

Jack pleaded for his life, the words so jumbled and fast she couldn't make them out. His fear stretched like a living thing across the distance, surrounding and suffocating her. Everything happened in an instant.

The smaller man aimed the gun at Jack's head and pulled the trigger.

She pressed both hands against her mouth. Hard. Neither man even glanced in her direction. They must have thought there was still a Dumpster behind the rickety privacy fence.

She recited the tale to Shane without revealing her arrest or the deal she'd made with WITSEC. Chances were, she'd have to be relocated and start all over again. She wanted Shane to remember the person she was now, not the person she'd been all those years ago.

"That's all of it," she said, her voice flat. "Turned out, the bald guy was Nick Amato, and he was a suspect in the shooting of a cop in Miami. Only they didn't have enough evidence to make it stick. They wanted him bad enough to make me a deal." As part of her agreement to testify and disappear, the shoplifting charges had disappeared, as well. "I entered the program. Earlier this year, Nick had a fatal heart attack. The marshals called a couple weeks later and said the threat level was deemed practically nonexistent. Technically, I can leave the program whenever I want. I even considered doing just that. Nothing would change but the designation on my file. The records remain sealed. My current identity stays in place. Nick was the only one who ever threatened me. End of story."

"What about the second guy?" Shane asked. "The one who was with Nick when Jack was shot."

"Nick tried to pin everything on him. Even claimed he was the shooter. Nick planted the gun in his car to sell the story. The police had him wiretapped, though. The guy wasn't too happy. In exchange for his testimony, the prosecutor lowered his sentence. If he wanted revenge on anyone, it would have been Nick."

There was no change in Shane's posture or demeanor. Instead of assuming his interrogation pose, he was relaxed back on his seat, his hands folded in his lap. A far cry from how he'd looked this morning.

That wasn't exactly fair. He'd appeared sympathetic, almost regretful, when he heard her story. Not that his opinion of her changed anything. Walt was gone and someone who had crawled out of the wreckage of her past life was responsible.

Shane's expression was intense, though she didn't think his interest was aimed at her. He appeared to be lost in thought.

"I spoke with the marshal this afternoon," he said after a lengthy pause. "Your contact in the program. He seemed confident there was no threat to you. I explained the situation and he said he'd check a few sources and get back to me. I haven't heard back from him yet."

She'd been transferred to Tom five years ago when her original contact retired. Nothing had altered much. Just the name and number she called when she needed to check in.

"Clearly, this changes everything." She indicated the postcard. "Someone knows something."

"Someone knows something. But who? That's the million-dollar question, isn't it? I've gone over the hotel guest list and the employee list. The ABI is going over it, as well. No one registered at or working at the resort has thrown up any red flags."

"What if he's not staying here?"

"There's a finite number of places to hide. There'd have to be a source of heat. There'd have to be water and supplies. Unless…"

"Unless he's got help."

"That would explain why no one in the hotel has raised any alarms." He wearily pinched the bridge of his nose with a thumb and forefinger. "I'll have security do another search of the outbuildings. Then I'll have the security footage reviewed once more. This place is covered with cameras. One of them must have picked up something."

"I just realized your only help is a passel of suspects."

"That occurred to me a while ago." He stifled a yawn. "Everyone is a suspect which means no one can be trusted. I've downloaded all the original footage for ABI to search. When I need the staff involved, I have them work in teams. If someone is trying to conceal something, that should make it more difficult."

"I see the problem."

Shane stopped the recording and slipped the phone into his pocket. "I'll give the marshal another call and let him know about the postcard. You've been in the program too long to slip up. There's a chance the leak came from the marshal's office. Stranger things have happened."

If there had been a leak in the marshals' office, did that make it better or worse? She'd been searching through the past few months of her life, trying to think of anything she might have said or done to reveal her identity. Nothing came to mind.

The only change had been Nick Amato's death which lowered her threat level. Even when she was considered at high risk, she'd only spoken with Tom once or twice a year when she checked in with him. Walt was the only one who knew about Nick's death besides the marshals.

A dull pain throbbed in her temples. There was no way Walt had anything to do with this. He knew the risk involved better than anyone.

Her headache grew worse. "Walt said the marshals didn't make mistakes."

"Everyone messes up."

That was an understatement. She hadn't stopped making mistakes in her life, but she'd tried to make fewer *stupid* mistakes. The kind of mistakes that got people arrested.

Her attention drifted to the mockingly cheerful postcard. She felt boneless and drained. She'd put on a good show, but seeing that card had bled the fight from her. First Jack and now Walt.

A nightmare thought struck her. What if something happened to Shane? At the moment he was the lone law-enforcement officer nearby.

He ran one hand along his beard and drew his fingers

to a point. "Maybe Nick had a relative no one knew about. Another son or a brother."

Her hands trembled and she curled them into fists.

"If he did," she said. "They never called him. They never wrote him a letter. The marshals monitored everyone who made contact with Nick while he was in prison. According to them, at the time of Nick's death, he hadn't had a visitor in over three years."

She massaged her temples. The questions just kept circling and circling. Walt had always been protective of her. Had the killer come for her and stumbled upon Walt instead? How much danger was Shane in?

"Well," he said, rubbing his eyes. "We're not going to figure it out tonight. The best thing we can both do is get some rest and tackle this in the morning with a clear head."

"Easier said than done."

"I know. I don't blame you for being scared. I'm doing everything I can to monitor the situation. I've got security in place. I doubt this guy will make a move without an escape plan, and that's at least another day out."

He did look exhausted. He was trapped here without any backup and carrying the weight of the world on his shoulders. Everyone in the borough depended on him.

Who did Shane lean on when he needed a break?

Adding to his burden, he had the safety of the people at the resort to think about. There'd been a slim chance the murderer hadn't taken refuge at the resort. The postcard changed everything.

Now they were faced with a resort full of suspects— any one of them could be the killer, and they were *all* in danger.

Shane's words kept ringing in her ears. *Is there anything you like about me?*

That was the problem—she liked *too much* about him. If her cover was blown, she'd have to start over again. That meant a new name and a new location. That meant leaving everything behind, including Shane.

The only way she'd have a secure future was by erasing the past completely once more. This was his home and his community. She couldn't drag him into the danger and uncertainty of her future. Their breakup was for the best and he deserved better. Except there was a heaviness in her chest that hadn't been there before.

He'd closed his eyes and rested the back of his head on the chair. On impulse, she circled around him and placed her hands on his shoulders.

His eyes startled open.

She swept one hand gently down his face, guiding them closed once more.

The space between them dissolved. She kneaded the tense muscles of his shoulders, then pressed her thumbs against the tight cords of his neck. He whistled a soft sigh through his teeth.

She slid her fingers into the soft strands of his hair and massaged his scalp. The scent of his hair teased her senses. He smelled like the outdoors, of winter days. She thought back to all the hours she'd spent on the dog sleds at Denali. There were days when she didn't see another person. Days when the dogs would curl up to rest and the only sound had been the wind whistling through the pine trees. Those had been good times. Peaceful times.

She slid her hands to his shoulders once more. His head was tipped back though he wasn't as relaxed as he appeared. There were lines around the edges of his mouth marking the quiet burden of concern he carried with him constantly.

He crossed one arm over his chest and caught her fingers, stilling her hand. "It's all right." He carefully tugged her around to stand before him. "You don't have to convince me of anything."

Her face heated and she stepped back. "I know how hard you're working. I'm sorry I didn't tell you that sooner."

He pushed himself to sit up straight. "It's been a long day for everyone."

"Yes."

Not since the trial had she told anyone about what happened to Jack that day. Even when Jack was facing death, he'd been looking out for her. He'd tried to protect her knowing he couldn't save himself. His final gesture had been one of sacrifice.

What had Walt been thinking in *his* final moment?

No matter how hard she tried, she couldn't hear his words. Just the echoes of his voice. She squeezed her eyes shut, willing her brain to recall something. Even a single word. Anything that might give them a sliver of a clue.

"There's something else. I'm not sure how to explain it."

She tried to wrap her head around what she wanted to say. She kept seeing Jack's face but Walt's voice. Why?

"What's that?" Shane nudged her.

"Walt and the other man were arguing." She closed her eyes. "It didn't sound as though either of them had the upper hand, you know?"

His forehead creased. "I'm not sure I do."

She opened and closed her hands, reaching for the right words. "When Nick was pointing the gun at Jack, he was confident. He was in control. Jack was scared. He was pleading."

Her voice caught and she bit the inside of her cheek to hold back the rush of emotion.

"I think I understand what you're saying," Shane said. "Walt's voice sounded angry instead of afraid."

"Exactly! Walt was mad, sure. But he didn't sound scared."

Then again, Walt had worked with the marshals at one time in his life. He'd had professional training in dealing with dangerous situations. Which still didn't explain the anger. She'd expect Walt to cajole or pacify—not escalate the situation.

"I'll make a note of what you said. It might be important for intent." Shane started toward the door, then stopped and pivoted. "Are you okay? You've been through a lot already, and that's a lot to dig up."

For a precious moment she allowed herself to imagine that things were different. That she was different. She allowed herself to imagine what it would be like to be loved by Shane. He embraced the town with his whole heart. What would it be like to have him love her the same way?

When she feared she was sinking too deep into the fantasy, she stepped away. "I'm tired."

The past was never really the past. That was the one constant in her life. Whenever it looked like things were going well, disaster struck. Shane was a part of her life she'd treasured, and she wanted to keep it that way. She didn't want to see his disappointment if he discovered the whole truth about her.

She'd already seen the doubt in his eyes when she spoke about the WITSEC program. The more they dug into her case, the more likely he was to find out about her own criminal history. She didn't want to risk losing

Shane's trust, not when they were trapped with limited resources.

"Rest is the best medicine," he said. "Is there anything I can get you? Anything you need?"

Though she hadn't seen Walt killed, when she closed her eyes, she pictured the scene from all those years ago—only it was Walt's face instead of Jack's.

She clasped her hands before her. "Would you stay until I fall asleep?"

Asking him was one of the hardest things she'd ever done. If he refused, she'd be humiliated. She held her breath, her heart beating as hard as it had when the killer was shooting at them.

"Yes," he replied.

Her pulse spiked. "Are you sure?"

"I'm sure. I've got about ten thousand emails to sort through on my phone. I needed a chance to catch up anyway."

She'd gotten herself worked up for nothing. There was no great concession on his part. He'd have been doing the same thing right next door. No wonder he'd agreed. Still, she appreciated his presence.

She crossed the room to the bedroom suite, then grasped the handle to close the door behind her. "Thank you."

"You're welcome."

The moment her head hit the pillow, she felt as though she was falling and falling and falling.

She'd survived a lot of things in her life, but she didn't know if she'd survive being the cause of Walt's death.

Shane lingered in the hallway outside Kara's door the following morning. She'd fallen asleep the previous evening almost immediately. He wasn't surprised. She was physically and emotionally drained. He'd arranged for security outside her door when he wasn't available.

Now that they had proof the killer was at the resort, the safety of Kara and the other guests was paramount. Though he believed Kara was the only target in true danger, he had a responsibility for everyone's safety. He'd spoken to his stepbrother and Graham had alerted the guests of the danger. They'd instructed the guests to use extra caution and to travel in pairs. Beyond that, there wasn't much more he could do.

The hotel security guard had brought a folding chair and a book and stationed himself facing the door. Shane recognized him from town as Ryan Redington, though everyone called him Red. He was in his thirties with a boyish face and a wispy ginger beard that he'd been trying to grow since he was nineteen.

Red flipped the page and glanced at Shane. "Do you need something?"

What did he need? Why was he still standing here?

"No, um, you've got my number if there's any trouble."

"Yep."

"Okay."

He was tired of operating on the defensive. Jeff had more resources back at the station, but Shane had been doing research on the computer in the business center. He'd wanted to see what he could dig up on Nick Amato and his "associate." See if there'd been any updates. Given his current isolation, he was operating on a trust-but-verify basis from now on.

The business center was located in a deserted wing off the first floor. In summer the cavernous room hosted retirement parties and wedding receptions. The business center was usually deserted. While guests liked to know they had a printer at their disposal, they rarely took advantage of the perk.

Shane was punching in the key code for the door when he caught a flash of movement from the corner of his eye. Keeping his head bent over the keypad, he pretended he hadn't noticed.

After counting to ten, he turned in the direction of the movement. Since he wasn't exactly light on his feet or inconspicuous, he decided to give whoever it was a head start.

He turned the corner and followed the hallway to the exit sign. He'd explored every inch of this hotel as a kid. While the security camera footage had been updated from video cassettes to DVDs to digital files, the layout was the same. There were plush carpeted hallways for the guests and tile corridors behind the scenes to make it easy to move staff and supplies discreetly from one end of the resort to the other.

Stepping through the metal door to the staff area was like entering a different world. The air was chilly instead of a comfortable seventy-two degrees, and his boots echoed off the tile instead of sinking into soft pile carpeting.

A serviceable open staircase led to the penthouse suites on the third floor and to the service corridors in the basement, one floor down.

While much of the rest of the building was covered by security cameras, he didn't spot any in the stairwell. There hadn't been any growing up, either. Something he and his friends had exploited more than once to sneak out.

Acting on instinct, he took the stairs down to the service corridors. The lights were on, and a rush of nostalgia took him by surprise. The hotel had been remodeled numerous times over the years. Down here, nothing had changed. The walls were painted the same industrial beige and the air had the same loamy basement scent he recalled from his youth.

Even the echo of his boots on the tile floor was familiar.

When he reached the center of the hotel there was a ramp to his right, which he knew led to the kitchen.

He turned left and took the stairs to the lobby. This area was the same. There was a security camera aimed at the front desk. Nothing covered the lobby exit.

This had been the best way to sneak out of the hotel when he was growing up. Back then, the cameras weren't quite as state-of-the-art as they were now, but they'd been in the same places.

Mark, the resort manager, glanced up. "May I help you, sir?" he inquired in a tone that indicated he'd like to do nothing of the sort.

"Did you see someone come through here a moment ago?"

"Yes."

"And?" Shane prodded. "Did you recognize the person?"

"I should hope so. It was my assistant, Marie. She was delivering sundries to one of the guests."

Sure enough, a slight woman in a maid's uniform appeared to the right of Mark and glanced at Shane expectantly.

"Is there something wrong, sir?"

"No. Nothing." He drummed his fingers on the counter. "Did you discover who left the envelope for Dr. Riley last evening, Mark?"

The corners of his mouth turned down. "No. There are blind spots in the hotel."

"You seem familiar with the blind spots."

"Most of the hotel employees grew up in town. Their parents worked here before them. I'd say almost everyone in Kodiak Springs is aware of the blind spots in this hotel." Mark bent his head and typed something onto the screen before him. "I recall hearing stories of your own exploits, Sergeant Taylor."

Shane bounced his fist off the counter. "The tales of my exploits are greatly exaggerated."

A slight smile appeared on the perpetually stoic manager's face. "I'm sure they are, sir."

Shane pivoted toward the stairs once more. What was wrong with him? He didn't have time to chase staff around the hotel. Dissolving into paranoia wasn't going to help anything.

Retracing his steps, he returned to the door for the staff exit once more and paused. There was still quite a bit of activity in the lobby. People drifted from the restaurant to the ornate bar. In warmth and safety, they watched as the blizzard raged outside the window. Edison bulb lights strung around the outdoor summer patio waved wildly in the wind.

He studied the myriad of faces, wondering who in the crowd might have a vendetta to settle. No one jumped out at him. They all looked wealthy and relaxed. Exactly as you'd expect someone to look at a seventeen-hundred-dollar-a-night resort.

He went back to the business center and typed his credentials into the computer. He sent an email to Jeff asking him to look up information in the national data exchange, then settled in for the long haul.

He spent the next two hours chasing links down endless rabbit holes. He'd done plenty of searches on Nick Amato already. Now he wanted to know more about the day of the killing.

The pad to his right was soon filled with pages of notes. He found nothing about Kara beyond a vague reference to a witness. True to their word, the DA had kept Kara's name out of the papers. The killing of a repo man in Florida fifteen years ago had barely rated a story on the third page of the *Florida Times-Union*.

There was, however, an interview with a woman who described herself as the deceased's girlfriend. Shane made a note of the name. Kara had mentioned that her mom had already broken up with Jack, but some people liked the attention of the news cameras. The woman had made a plea for donations to cover the cost of funeral expenses. There were no pictures of the funeral. If there had been, would he have found Kara in the crowd? What had she looked like, all those years ago? How much had she changed?

She was still holding something back. He didn't need his detective skills to realize Kara was ashamed of her past.

There was nothing new to discover about Nick Amato. He'd been nothing more than a low-level thug for most of his life. Several untimely deaths had moved him up the ranks until he controlled most of the sketchier neighborhoods in Jacksonville.

Nick had kept a fairly low profile until a dustup in Miami. An undercover cop had been killed in the crossfire of a turf war. Just like that, Nick had gone from lowlife to the big time. He eluded arrest for five years before his son's car was repossessed—with a number of stolen guns in the trunk.

Shane jumped to the story of Nick's funeral, which only "a handful of mourners attended." He studied the scattering of faces. It appeared as though only a couple of reporters had covered it.

On a hunch, he searched for the name of the woman who'd claimed she was Jack's girlfriend at the time of his death. The one who'd been collecting donations for the funeral. Six months after Jack's murder, one Ms. Elena Williams pled guilty to felony theft by conversion after the money she'd collected never actually found its way to the funeral home.

He'd seen a lot of despicable people in his time as a trooper, and even he was shocked by people who stole in the name of the dead.

The woman was given two years in prison and eight months' probation. That might explain why Kara had been willing to enter the program alone at such a young age. If Ms. Williams was her mother, she didn't sound like much of a parent.

Shane added the information about Ms. Williams to his growing stack of notes. With a yawn, he arched his back and stretched, lifting his fisted hands above his head.

For old time's sake, when he left the business center he took the tunnel again. Everything he'd learned over the past few days had made him melancholy. Maybe it was time to sweep some of the cobwebs out of his head. He wasn't a kid anymore. He wasn't powerless. Any echoes of his childhood were just that—echoes.

He'd crafted a life where he was in control at all times. He did his best at his job, and when things didn't turn out the way he wanted, he let it go. Most things, anyway. Some calls stayed with him. Mostly the domestic disturbance calls. They always came from the same houses. He always went through the same procedures. He always said the same prayers.

At least he was there to defuse the situations. The people he worried most about were the ones who didn't make the call.

At the bottom of the steps, he hesitated. Maybe he'd swing by the kitchen and see if he could snatch a dessert, like he'd done when he was a kid. He knew just where cake was stored.

He'd made it as far as the landing when the corridor was plunged into darkness. His senses on alert, he reached for the flashlight on his utility belt.

Footsteps pounded and he turned toward the noise. His flashlight illuminated a cone of area before him. A muzzle flash and a blast sounded the instant before the wall exploded near his head.

A sharp pain stung his cheek and he dove away. A second gunshot reverberated through the corridor. Gauging his route purely on instinct, he jogged forward, then ducked into a narrow alcove.

Feeling like a rat in a maze, he unholstered his weapon. Without a clear line of sight, he wasn't risking a blind shot.

Footsteps sounded again and he exited the safety of the alcove. The echoes of his own boots along with his harsh breathing made it difficult to hear anything else.

The pop of a third gunshot indicated the shooter was moving away from him. Keeping low, he pressed his flashlight against the wall and used it to gauge his direction.

When he reached a second alcove, he groped along the wall until he found the switch plate. The sudden shock of light temporarily blinded him. His gun outstretched, he searched the area. He crept forward and peered up the open staircase.

A door slammed in the distance. His blood racing, he pounded his flashlight against the wall in frustration. There was no way he'd be able to catch up. Even knowing it was futile, he searched the stairway before all the thoughts fled from his head but one: *Kara.*

NINE

Kara had showered, dressed and finished breakfast when a fierce pounding on the door nearly made her leap out of her skin.

She peered through the peephole and saw Shane.

"All right already," she muttered as she opened the door. "Where's the fire?"

He glanced behind her. "Is everything okay?"

She caught sight of the security guard's bewildered face.

"I'm fine," she said. "Did you think I wouldn't be? What's going on?"

"Someone took a shot at me."

Her stomach dipped and she noticed a scratch on his cheek. "You're hurt!"

He swiped at the spot and turned toward Red. "Have you seen anyone, anyone at all in the past fifteen minutes?"

"No. Nothing." Red shook his head. "What now?"

Shane slumped against the wall and braced his hands on his legs. "I'll stay with Kara. I need you to check the security footage from the north stairwell, then ask around and see if anyone saw anything unusual. Even though the shooting happened in the basement, sound will have carried. Let Graham know what's happening."

His face pale, Red stood. "I'll get right on it."

"Let me know immediately if you find anything," Shane said.

From his expression, she guessed his thoughts. "You don't expect him to find anything, do you?"

He tipped his head back. "No. Whoever it was shut off the lights. We're not going to see anything more than a couple of muzzle flashes."

She sank weakly onto a chair. "Why shoot at you?"

"I surprised him. I was using the employee corridors. I doubt he expected to see me there."

"Do you think it was an employee?"

"Maybe. Maybe not. I'd expect to see an employee in the employee corridors. Why hide? Unless it was someone who wasn't supposed to be there."

"I guess."

He straightened. "Say, you haven't seen the dogs since we got here. Do you feel up to a visit now?"

"After everything you just went through? Is it safe?"

"If the shooter is smart, he won't risk another attack. Not this soon. Not with everyone in the hotel about to be alerted. And this guy doesn't strike me as dumb."

She tested her leg with a little more weight, pleased to discover there was barely a twinge. She had been wanting to check on the dogs.

"As long as you're sure you're okay."

"I'm sure." He shook out his hands. "What else is there to do? We're not any safer here. By now, he probably knows where your room is anyway. Being unpredictable is the best defense. I need to get out of this hotel for a while. Get a change of scenery. It's starting to get to me."

She understood exactly what he was saying and her heart went out to him. Unburdening the story of Jack's murder had shifted something inside her. She'd thought the only way to let Jack go was by forgetting him, yet he'd only loosened his hold on her when she'd spoken of him.

Sometimes getting some distance from the problem was the best way to gain perspective.

"Then let's go." She turned toward the closet. "I need some fresh air."

She pulled on her boots and donned her coat. She didn't have any gloves but maybe there was a pair in the lost and found. She'd check when they passed by the front desk.

Her phone rang. She glanced at the screen. The number wasn't familiar. Probably someone in search of a vet.

"Hello," she said.

There was a low whistling sound. Almost like wind. She pressed the phone tighter to her ear and heard an odd, staticky rumbling, like someone was handling the phone.

"Is anyone there?"

Shane glanced at her in question and she shrugged her shoulders. She expected to hear someone talk and nearly spoke again before an unexpected impulse made her clamp her mouth shut.

The sudden silence chilled her to the bone.

She closed her eyes, willing herself to be quiet. For a moment, she thought she heard the faint whisper of someone breathing. A chill of alarm spread through her body and sent the blood pounding in her ears.

"Who is this?" she demanded.

"Oh, sorry," a man spoke. His voice was faint and breathless, as though he was walking. "It's Finn. We talked earlier. In the dining room. Do you remember what we talked about?"

"Yes."

"Don't tell Mark we spoke."

"The manager? Why?"

"I can't talk. Not over the phone. Just be careful around him, all right?"

"Wait," she began, but the line went dead.

"Who was that?" Shane asked.

"That was Finn. He said to be careful around Mark. I'm going to call him back."

"Why should you be careful around the manager?"

"That's what I'd like to know."

The line rang several times before going to voice mail.

Shane pulled out his phone. "I don't like this. We'll have to postpone the trip to the kennels, and Red can review the security footage later. We need to track down Finn."

The guard was back outside her door in minutes, his chest heaving. He must have jogged the distance.

He had a youthful-looking face that Kara guessed disguised his true age. The ginger beard he was unsuccessfully trying to grow made him look younger rather than older. He wore civilian clothing, but she'd caught a glimpse of a gun holster beneath his leather bomber jacket.

Red glanced between the two of them. "What's wrong? What's happened?"

"We need to check on a geologist staying at the hotel," Shane said. "The guy's name is Finn… What's his last name?" He directed the question to Kara.

"Only one guy named Finn staying here," Red declared before she could answer. "Room 112."

The three of them set off for the elevator.

Shane turned to her. "Follow my instructions when we get there, okay? No questions."

She bristled. "No questions."

Her annoyance lasted until she caught sight of the lines of fatigue creasing the edges of his mouth. Maybe it was time to cut Shane a little slack. He hadn't ordered her to stay behind, after all. He was always being forced to leave her alone or risk putting her in danger. The least she could do was stay out of his way.

A few people gave them quizzical looks as they rushed through the lobby and down the opposite corridor. Her leg was protesting by the time they reached the wing where Finn's room was located. He was on the first floor, several doors down from the lobby.

When they reached the room, Shane motioned for her and Red to stay back. He gave a sharp rap on the door and called out Finn's name.

When no one answered, Red stepped forward. He used his master key card to unlock the door, then moved protectively in front of Kara.

Shane turned to Red. "Does it look like this is a crisis that may require immediate intervention?"

Red didn't hesitate. "That's my take."

Kara glanced between the two men. "What are you guys talking about?"

"Fourth Amendment," Shane said. "I'm not allowed to search a hotel room without a warrant unless there are exigent circumstances."

"I'd say this counts," she readily agreed.

His gun drawn, Shane cautiously entered the room. With each passing second, her nerves grew. After a tense few minutes, he stepped out once more and motioned to Kara and Red.

"It's clear," he said, his chin set in a hard line. "He's not in there, and nothing looks out of place."

Red brushed past him and looked inside. Kara peered beneath his arm. The room was neat and tidy. The bed was made. There was no clothing on the floor, no soda cans or discarded dishes cluttering the tables. Nothing to mark an extended stay. His papers were stacked neatly on the desk.

"Stay here." Shane directed the statement at her. "We're on shaky legal ground already."

While the two men searched, Kara paced outside in the corridor. They didn't locate Finn's phone or computer. The front desk was searching through security footage to see if they could find him.

The walls felt like they were closing in around her. Instead of a cozy getaway, the luxury resort was a trap. The corridors were mazes filled with places to hide. Wrapping her arms around her body, she shivered.

Shane stepped out. "The staff is canvassing the hotel. Someone thought they saw him heading toward the outdoor spring. I'm going to check it out."

"Let me come," she said. "You need all the eyes you can get right now."

He hesitated, then turned to Red. "What did they say at the front desk?"

"Finn was picked up on camera last night. He was in the dining room, seated next to another guest. Maybe she knows something."

"She doesn't." Kara lifted her hand. "The other guest was me."

"That takes care of that," Red said, checking his phone

again. "Okay. He was in the dining room this morning. We're checking the conference rooms. I guess he works there sometimes."

"Anything else?"

"Someone saw him at the outdoor pool earlier, but he isn't there now," Red said. "According to the staff on duty, no one has gone outside recently."

"Red, why don't you help search the hotel?" Shane said, his thumbs hitched in his utility belt. "Kara, you're with me. We'll see if he spoke to anyone. See if anyone can help us track his movements."

She nodded. "What do you think?"

"I don't know what to think." His voice went quiet and flat. "There's nothing to indicate anything is wrong. Still, I'd feel better if we could track him down."

"You and me both."

Her interest in visiting the outdoor pool was twofold. She wanted to see if they could track down Finn, but she also wanted to check on the dogs. The outdoor pool was on the way to the kennels. While she understood the uncertainty of the situation, she also had an obligation to the animals under her care. Once they found Finn, she might still be able to sneak in a visit. As they crossed through the hotel, a fine sheen of sweat formed under her coat. She unzipped the collar to cool down. They followed the path through the resort and the enclosed walkway. Steam rolled out of the indoor pool enclosure the moment Shane opened the door. Unlike the natural pool outside, this swimming area was completely man-made. Mediterranean-blue tiles lined the walls, and a zero-entry ramp sloped into the warm mineral waters. A dozen or so guests swam lazily or lounged in the pool while the weather stormed outside. Plush robes and lambswool slippers awaited their exit.

Two uniformed attendants circulated around the room. One held a tray of sparkling water and the other straightened a stack of impossibly fluffy white towels. Earlier she'd joked about Finn stealing a towel. After seeing what was available in the spa, the joke didn't seem so farfetched. One resort towel probably cost more than all the towels she owned put together.

As many times as she'd been to the resort to check on the sled dogs, there were still times when the juxtaposition with life in the town had caught her off guard.

A door on the far side of the indoor pool led to a chute-like covered walk to the hot springs outside. Weather permitting, the heartier souls donned their swimsuits and braved the freezing weather to jump into the warm water. The tradition was affectionately known as the "arctic plunge."

Shane conferred with one of the attendants to ensure none of them had seen Finn before they went out. After the warmth of the indoor pool enclosure, the shock of winter air took her breath away. She quickly zipped her coat again. She'd forgotten to check the front desk for gloves, so she stuffed her hands in her pockets. The snow had relented some, but the wind still howled through the covered walkway.

She sure didn't plan on participating in the arctic plunge anytime soon.

Enormous boulders edged the natural pool. An open boardwalk illuminated by hanging Edison bulbs circled the pool. The water was inky black with feathery steam floating from the surface. Snowflakes collided with the hot water and immediately melted.

Kara pointed. "I'll go that direction. You go the other way. We'll meet at the far side."

Shane hesitated.

She gave him a gentle shove. "You can see me. The faster we search, the sooner we get back inside."

"All right."

The path hadn't been cleared recently, and the ankle-deep snow stung where her boots ended and her jeans began. She spotted depressions in the snow and scooted around them. They might be footprints, but she couldn't tell for certain. Wind and snow had already eroded them. By the time she reached the south end of the pool, not twenty feet away from the door, her face was numb and her hands tingled. Her bandaged leg protested the cold. She limped forward and peered over the edge.

There was no sign of Finn and no indication he'd been there recently. She was turning back when a flash of something pale caught her attention. She stepped off the path and leaned over one of the jagged boulders that flanked the pool. The freezing surface of the rock penetrated even through her down coat, and she winced.

She squinted into the dark water. The faint light from the path barely reached beyond the boardwalk. That was when she spotted him. Finn's dark sweater was unmistakable.

Her stomach twisted. He was floating facedown, his head and shoulders visible.

"Shane!" she hollered. "I found him!"

She tipped forward, reaching out one arm. By stretching as far as she could, her fingertips brushed over the material of his sweater. His body was unnaturally still and cold, and she stifled a gag.

Her leg ached and she'd extended far enough that the

toe of her boot lifted off the ground. She was so close. She retracted her hand and hoisted her upper body farther up the rock surface, then scooched forward on the ledge. Her lungs burned at the exertion.

The extra distance allowed her to grasp Finn's sweater. The material was icy cold, and snow was clumping on the surface. She tugged. He didn't budge. She tugged again. The body was too heavy, and she was overleveraged on the lip of the rock.

As she reached for a third time, something pushed against her foot, propelling her forward. The material of her coat glided over the icy surface. Flattening her hands, she tried to slow her descent. The sharp edges of the boulder scraped her bare palms. With a horrified shriek, she plunged headfirst into the water.

Instantly disoriented, her hands flailed, and she caught the dead man's arm. Water soaked into her coat and her heavy boots sucked her down.

She slipped deeper. Kicking desperately, she pushed toward the surface. Her heart pounded and her lungs screamed for air. Unable to see anything in the inky, black water, she thrashed around. Her fingers brushed against the slippery rock wall. There was nothing to grab. Nothing to hold. She sank beneath the surface and panic clawed through her.

She was drowning.

The surface of the water bubbled, and Shane caught a glimpse of Kara's pale hand.

He circled her wrist and heaved her above the surface. She gasped and clawed at his arm.

Though weighted by her saturated coat, he managed to haul her out of the water. He lifted her against his chest. The warm water steamed as it met the frigid temperatures.

She strained away from him. "It's Finn. We have to help him."

"No." He strode toward the indoor enclosure. "We can't help him."

"We have to," she demanded, her eyes wild and unfocused.

"Kara, listen to me. You're wet." He spoke calmly, keeping her tightly against his chest. "We need to go inside."

Moisture seeped through his gloves.

"What if…"

"We can't save him. It's too late."

He didn't know if it was his words or the sharp snowflakes peppering her face, but something must have permeated the fog of her panic because she suddenly stilled.

She lifted her stricken gaze to him. "We can't leave him."

"I'll take care of him," Shane said gently. "I promise. But I have to take care of you first."

Her face was ashen, and her teeth chattered. He'd known immediately that Finn was dead. Kara probably had too; the shock of the past few days was just wearing on her.

When they returned inside, one of the attendants glanced up from folding a stack of towels. He took one look at the water dripping from Kara's coat and immediately straightened.

The man gestured toward a bank of doors. "The dressing rooms are equipped with showers. I'll find some dry clothes."

"Call the front desk. Tell him we need a security team at the mineral pools."

Kara reached out a hand. "Did anyone else come in or out that door?"

"No." The attendant replied. "No one. I've been here the whole time."

Shane adjusted her in his arms. "Let's get you warm and then you can tell me what that was all about."

The tiled shower of the dressing room featured a bench and Shane carefully set her down. He turned on the shower and worked her free from her coat. The water soon warmed, and he moved her beneath the spray.

A discreet knock signaled the arrival of the attendant with a stack of clothing in his outstretched hand.

Shane recognized the soft pink-and-gray plaid from the hotel spa. "Thanks."

"There's a pair of slippers on the bottom and a robe on the hook by the door."

The man turned and pulled the door closed.

Kara huddled beneath the warm shower. Some of the color had returned to her cheeks.

"Okay," he said. "What happened?"

She caught his gaze. "I think someone pushed me."

"Are you sure? I didn't see anyone."

"I didn't either. But I felt something."

He stabbed his hand through his hair. "I shouldn't have brought you. I thought you'd be safe. How could he have known where we were in time to lie in wait? I don't get it."

"I don't know. Maybe I imagined it. Everything happened so fast."

"Or maybe you didn't. Maybe he saw us leave."

"But how did he get to the pool without anyone seeing him?"

"We have to search your room. There's a chance he's been listening to us. How else could he follow us so quickly?"

Steam filled the room. He didn't know what to think. Kara hadn't been out of his sight for long. He didn't see how someone could come upon her so fast without being seen. Was there a chance she had imagined the push?

She swiped the moisture from her face. "I must have imagined it." She looked as though she might say more, then waved him toward the door. "I'm fine. There are a dozen people outside that door. I'm safe, for now. Go. I'll get changed and be right out."

He paced outside the door. Finn had warned Kara about the manager, Mark.

Shane searched the faces of the people who were gathering their belongings to leave.

He touched the sleeve of one of the workers. "Write down the name of everyone who was in here just now. Guests and employees."

"Yes, sir," the man replied.

He'd question them all. Someone had to have seen something.

When Kara reappeared a short time later, her hair was wrapped in a towel and a fluffy robe was belted around her waist. Slippers monogrammed with the resort insignia peeked from beneath the hem.

She looked warm and dry and impossibly beautiful.

He tugged the edges of her robe beneath her chin and held them snugly. She wrapped her arms around his waist and held him tightly. His hands were pressed between them. He tucked his head into the crook of her neck, savoring the feel of her. He didn't know who was comforting whom in that moment.

He only knew that she was soft and alive, and against all odds she smelled like cherry blossoms. She felt incredibly fragile in that moment.

Kara pulled away first. Her fingers were icy cold, and he massaged them between his. When Red opened the door, she clasped the back of Shane's head and pressed their foreheads together.

"Go," she ordered quietly. "You have work to do."

He started to leave, then pressed a kiss against her knuckles. "Are you sure you're all right?"

"I'm fine." She gestured toward a chair. "I'm going to stay near, if you don't mind. I'm not ready to be alone just yet."

"I'm not letting you out of my sight. Holler if you need anything."

"I promise."

That nagging sensation returned, the feeling that something wasn't quite right. How long had Finn been in the water? Kara mentioned he'd been preoccupied with the cameras.

The computer at the front desk could pull up any of the digital feeds at any time. There were at least four people, possibly five, who had access to the stored security files. If someone wanted to alter something or to erase something, they had the means at their disposal.

He mentally ticked off the people he knew for certain had access. There was Red and the second full-time security guard, Pete. Then there were Graham and Mark. They could erase movements and they'd know all the blind spots in the system. All of them had the means, but what would be the motive?

Red approached him. His gaze skittered to Kara, then back again.

"What is it? What's happening?"

Shane drew him away and explained the circumstances. They decided to wait for the second security guard before they attempted to secure the body.

While Red paced and tried to steel himself to deal with his first dead body, Shane calculated his options.

Nearly forty-eight hours had gone by, and the winds hadn't yet died down enough to bring in the helicopter. The longest he'd ever seen a storm like this last was three days. If the road wasn't cleared by tomorrow, at least they'd have a helicopter.

Jeff was standing by with a team of enforcement officers he'd recruited from nearby towns. They were prepared to make the trip on snow machines first thing the next day. They'd considered making an attempt immediately, but the weather had turned them back.

When Pete arrived, they left him to watch over Kara while he and Red stepped out into the cold. When they finally managed to get Finn inside, they placed him on the floor and Red covered him with one of the towels. The moment the body was covered, Red leaned over, his hands on his knees. Shane heard his deep, heaving breaths. He turned away to give Red a moment to gather himself.

Pete didn't look much better, but at least he was upright. He offered to retrieve the stretcher that was kept in the snow machine shed for emergencies. Shane was more than happy to let him go.

While they awaited his return, Graham pushed through the door and took in the scene.

His face paled. "Is that…? Is he…?"

Shane nodded and gave him the abbreviated version of events leading up to Kara discovering Finn.

Graham listened carefully, then seemed to gather himself. "Do you know what happened? I told him to be careful around the pools." He yanked on his collar. "I can't believe this."

Shane cleared his throat. "I don't think this was an accident."

Graham seemed uncertain for a moment, as though he was trying to figure out what could have happened if Finn's death hadn't been an accident.

Shane noted when the explanation dawned on him.

Graham fisted his hand against his mouth. "Oh no. Do you think this has something to do with what happened to Walt?"

"Has to be. We need to increase the security for the rest of the guests. We'll have additional law enforcement here tomorrow if I have to drag them up here myself. Until then, we have to deal with short staffing overnight. This is a suspicious death and we have to consider the safety of the remaining resort guests."

"Are you sure that he was…he was…that someone did this to him?"

"I can't be certain of anything. But it doesn't look good."

"Okay." Graham nervously smoothed his hair. "What needs to happen next?"

Shane explained that he was going to give a shelter-in-place order that would start after dinner and last overnight. With everyone confined to their rooms, they'd have an easier time tracking people's movements on the security cameras.

Graham absorbed the instructions and Shane could see him working out how best to implement them.

When they'd agreed on the plan, Shane asked, "What can you tell me about Finn? How well did you know him?"

Graham braced the knuckles of one hand on his hip and palmed the back of his head. "I didn't know him that well. He kept to himself. He had some sort of grant from the University of Anchorage to study the hot springs. See what kind of organisms or plants or something could live in the heat."

"Was there anyone in the hotel he was friendly with? An employee or another one of the guests?"

"Not that I know of, but I'll ask around. I'd see him in the lounge on his computer a lot. He may have gotten to know one of the guests there."

"What about the employees? Any friends?"

"No. Like I said. He kept to himself."

"How long has he been staying here?"

"A couple of weeks. He did some research in town first. You know, studying how the Native Alaskans used the hot springs. That sort of thing."

"And his room was comped."

"Absolutely. No way the university could afford it. I figured we'd get some good publicity once he published his paper. I was going to get a news team up here for a human-interest story."

"Do you have an emergency contact for him?"

"I don't know. Probably. I'll check. I'll get in touch with the university if I can't find anything."

"The weather has to break sooner or later. Jeff will have a forensics team on the chopper first thing when it does. He's also coordinating more officers to make the trip cross-country. We'll take statements from each of the guests and coordinate an effort to get everyone out. Most of them should be checking out over the weekend, right?"

"Yeah. We close the week after next until the start of the summer season." Graham heaved a sigh. "I'm on a plane to California as soon as we do. I'm ready for some sun. I'm ready for the beach." His gaze sharpened. "Wait. Should I stick around?"

"Depends. Who's staying behind?"

"Red and Pete, the other security guard, will keep watch on the place. After this fiasco, I don't plan on offering winter packages again, that's for sure. I'm going to spend the season in California and let someone else deal with the cold. And the avalanches. And whatever else this state decides to throw at them."

Shane sympathized with the sentiment. He didn't recall ever being this tired or stretched this thin. He was going to sleep for a week when this was all over. Tomorrow couldn't come soon enough. He'd finally have his forensics team. He'd finally have additional officers to question the guests.

He'd also be able to get Kara out of here and secure. He glanced over to where she was sitting. She'd curled up in the chair, her head bent. After all she'd been through the past couple of days, she deserved a little peace. He hoped she was finding some, if only for a few hours. They'd have plenty more to worry about tomorrow when the law enforcement teams descended on the resort.

"Before you leave," Graham said, interrupting his thoughts, "I need you to be truthful with me. Like, completely and totally honest. How much danger am I putting these guests in? I need to know."

Walt and now Finn. What was the link? If this was

all connected to Kara, then how did Finn fit into the picture? Had he seen or heard something the day he'd spoken with Walt?

"I honestly don't know," Shane said. "An hour ago, I'd have said the threat to the guests was low. After this, I'm not certain."

"And my employees? How hard are you looking at them?"

"They're getting the same treatment as everyone else. Until we know what happened, everything is on the table."

"C'mon." Graham's shoulders curled forward, and he stuffed his hands into his pockets. "You've known these people your whole life. I've been living in this town since I was a kid. People get in trouble, sure. But not like this. I can't see it. I can't see anyone on my staff doing something like this."

Much as it pained him, Shane was considering everyone who'd been at the resort this weekend, including Graham. The crimes in Kodiak Springs were generally centered around alcohol and drug abuse, and he knew the names and addresses of all the repeat offenders in town. People, he'd learned over the years, were capable of almost anything.

"I'm doing my due diligence, that's all. It's nothing personal."

Graham rolled his shoulders back, relaxing his defensive stance. "I appreciate you being straight with me. I'll inform the guests. Knowing that we'll have help tomorrow should alleviate most of the worry."

"The guests will have to leave as soon as the road is cleared. It's not safe until we find the killer."

"I'll work with the front desk and coordinate travel arrangements."

"Good. One more thing. Did Finn ever mention Walt?"

"No." Graham tilted his head to one side. "Why would Finn mention Walt?"

"It's nothing." Shane waved him off. "I'm following through on everything. I heard they were both history buffs."

"Finn was here for research, and that included the history around here. If they knew each other, that's probably where they'd met."

"What about Mark? Was there any animosity between the two men?"

Graham snorted. "Other than that Mark looks down on anyone who isn't a millionaire or billionaire? Finn didn't like being treated like a second-class citizen, but Mark's priorities are the paying guests."

Unless there was something more. "Make certain Finn's room is sealed," Shane said. "There might be evidence."

"Okay."

Graham left to inform the guests while Shane and Red took care of the body. Pete stayed behind with Kara. The resort had a cooler for big game that was used in the summer and sat empty over the winter. They ensured the door was locked before returning to the indoor pool.

Once the body was secured, they searched outside for any evidence, though there wasn't much hope of finding anything as long as the storm circled around them. They returned inside and scrutinized every inch of the pool house.

Soon they'd peeled off their jackets and rolled up their sleeves in deference to the heat of the room. Their careful search revealed nothing. There was a security camera focused on the pool and one pointed at the door leading to the resort. There was nothing trained on the exit to the outdoor pool. Shane requested the security footage. This time he asked Pete along with two other employees. Though having the files viewed with a team wasn't a foolproof way to ensure no one altered the footage, it was the only option he had at the moment.

Shane kept an eye on Kara and watched as the warmth lulled her into a restless slumber. She turned to one side, then turned again. After about forty minutes, her restless movements stilled. She tucked her legs beneath her, pressed her hands together as though in prayer, and rested her cheek against her fingers. Soon she was breathing evenly, her chest rising and falling in the regular rhythm.

She was unguarded in her sleep, her lips gently parted. Not for the first time he realized how rigidly she held herself when she was awake. The life she'd led had left her guarded and untrusting. Not that he blamed her for the defensive measures she'd put in place to protect herself.

He swiped at the perspiration dotting his forehead. My, but she was beautiful. A series of memories played through his head like a film reel of the time they'd spent together. He lingered over the recollections of her strength and humor and compassion. Her quiet contemplation and the way her brow creased in worry.

He'd chased bears out of his garage and disarmed a man trying to stab him with less trepidation than he felt when facing this slip of a woman who'd burrowed into his heart.

Except love exacted too high a price. He'd seen the destructive power up close. He'd seen what his mother was willing to endure, what she was willing to suffer, in the name of love. He refused to be a victim. He'd seen how easily someone could be manipulated when strong feelings were involved.

When he was with Kara, he was happy. Then, just as quickly, he'd feel out of control. He was afraid and guilty for feeling that way. He'd accused Kara of always expecting the worst from him, but hadn't he been guilty of doing the same thing to her?

When they were dating, he'd felt like nothing he'd done was right. He'd looked for her approval, as though seeking her permission to exist in the relationship. He'd been burdening her with his own insecurities without ever recognizing what he was doing.

Growing up he'd instinctively known that what was happening in his house was wrong. Loving someone meant protecting them, not harming them. He'd been furious with his mom for her dependence on an abusive relationship. He'd been furious with her for putting them both in harm's way, and he'd punished himself for being unable to protect either of them.

He'd been looking to Kara to give him the strength and grace to love. He'd set her an impossible task, and when she'd failed, he'd retreated back into his old habits. Those habits had served him well in the past. There was no reason to doubt them now.

He'd seen healing as another lie. As another way to cover up the truth. Though he believed his dad's epiphany after his mother's death, he didn't trust that the changes in him were permanent. Sometimes Shane even wondered if his dad was sincere. His dad sometimes acted as though his life leading up to his wife's death had proved to be counterproductive, so he'd done something else. Had there been any true growth and healing?

Shane had thought boxing up the memories was the best way to move forward. Instead, he'd dragged them along with him without ever realizing what he'd done. Not until now, anyway.

Kara's eyes blinked open and she smiled tenderly at him. "How long have I been asleep?"

"Not long," he said, swallowing around the lump in his throat.

She sat up, then stretched and yawned, arching her back as she reached toward the ceiling. "You look tired."

"I am," he replied.

His instinct had been to lie. To reassure her that he was fine. That he wasn't tired. That he was invincible, and it was important that everyone around him know it, as well. Instead, he'd told the truth. That one simple act released something inside him, and he felt lighter.

She touched his cheek, her fingers gliding along the shaggy length of his beard. "You should get some rest."

The tightness in his chest wasn't so bad this time around.

He placed his fingers over hers. "All right."

Though exhausted, he had no plans to rest. Not until the killer was found and Kara was safe. The sooner he got her away from here, the better.

Whether or not she'd ever return was another matter.

TEN

Kara pushed open the door to the kennels and let the familiar sights and smells wash over her like a soothing balm. She never ceased to be amazed by the lavish kennels at the resort. Each individual stall had a flap door leading to the outside. The center aisle was tiled, and the floor was heated. Everything was scrupulously clean and the metal glimmered. Sled dogs were as much of a tourist attraction as the hot springs and the northern lights, which she supposed accounted for their comfortable digs.

She was desperate for a change of scenery. Even the air circulating through the ducts had started to feel stale. She'd also been washing and wearing the same outfit.

Shane had reluctantly agreed to let her visit the kennels, as long as he was allowed to escort her. He was currently prowling the outside of the building to make certain all the doors were locked tight. She appreciated his concern, though she'd be grateful when this was all over.

Her parka was hopelessly ruined from her dousing, and the one the resort had lent her was a size too big.

Finn's death had shaken her more than she'd realized. She kept flashing back to their conversation in the dining room. He'd been nervous and jittery, but he hadn't seemed particularly afraid. If she'd done something different, if she'd said something different…would he still be here?

Had someone actually pushed her into the pool, or had she imagined it?

The questions haunted her.

One of the dogs spotted her, and soon all the dogs were barking. The racket drew Trisha from the stall at the far end of the kennels that she'd repurposed for a makeshift office.

Trisha was in her midtwenties with jet-black hair that she wore in a long braid that dusted her belt loops. She'd taken over management of the kennels a few months before, and Kara was pleased with her work. Firm but compassionate, she was ideally suited for the task. If she hadn't been working here, Kara would have recruited her to work with her at the clinic in town.

When the weather was clear in the winter, the guests took rides through the surrounding woods. In the summer, the dogs were loaded into trucks and transported up to the glacier at Da'nai Pass. Winter or summer, no trip to the hot springs was complete without a sled dog ride.

Trisha smiled in greeting. "I heard you got trapped at the hotel because of the avalanche. Walt's dogs will be glad to see you."

Leaning over the enclosure, Kara patted one of her more enthusiastic greeters. "I figured I better check on Zoya's pups. How are they doing?"

"I'd say they're doing fantastic considering they're a winter litter. Zoya is a good mama."

"And Snowball? He's the runt."

"He's not as active as the others, but I haven't been

overly concerned with his progress. Probably wouldn't hurt for you to take a look at him."

"I thought I'd sit with them awhile."

"Be my guest. I was just locking up." Trisha extended her hand, passing over the key. "You can shut off the lights and lock the door when you leave."

"Will do," Kara replied.

She made her way down the center of the kennels, pausing to pet each dog in turn. The sled dogs were as smart as they were jealous, and she made sure to give each of them equal amounts of time and praise.

While she was uncertain in other areas of her life, she was confident in her ability with animals.

She'd always had a sixth sense where they were concerned, even when she was a kid. Her mom had never allowed her to have a pet. They were too expensive and too much work, she'd insisted. Kara had tended to the neighborhood strays, instead. She prided herself on winning over even the most suspicious of the scruffy mongrels.

Now that she'd greeted all the dogs, the puppies monopolized her attention.

Zoya lifted her head and eyed Kara suspiciously before lying on her side once more. She appeared more than ready for bed, while the five puppies bounded around her and nipped at her ears and tail.

When they caught sight of Kara, they clumsily trotted over, grateful for a new playmate. She left the door to the enclosure open, then tossed the blanket she'd brought onto the tile floor.

Shane stepped through the door and stomped the snow from his feet. Once he'd secured the lock, Kara patted the space on the blanket beside her.

One of the puppies immediately took the invitation and scampered over.

"Come and sit down. You need some puppy therapy."

He doffed his hat and lowered himself to the ground, stretching out his legs before crossing his ankles.

Kara swept the shaggy hair from his forehead. "You're starting to look scruffy."

He self-consciously smoothed the strands. "I know."

"I like it."

If she didn't know better, she'd have thought her comment made him blush.

There was nothing she could do right then about Walt or Finn or anything else beyond the doors, so she decided to enjoy the quiet moment. Walt had been surprised and proud of the unexpected litter. They were mostly cream and brown, some of them already showing the distinct face markings of a malamute.

Snowball toddled over to her on unsteady legs. He looked like he'd been taking a nap and hadn't fully awakened yet.

"That's Snowball," Kara said. "He's the runt of the litter, the one I've been worried about."

Shane reached out a hand and scratched Snowball behind his ears. "He looks pretty good to me."

"That little guy is a survivor."

She had a soft spot in her heart for the little fighter. She'd been there when he first entered the world. He'd been smaller than the rest and weaker. She and Walt had supplemented his feedings when the other puppies were too aggressive, shoving him out of the way.

He was also the only one of the pups who was a pure cream color with no markings. Even with his difficult beginnings, he was curious and friendly.

The puppy sniffed Shane's boots. Zoya lumbered to the door of the kennel to assess the new person. When she'd investigated Shane, she turned three times in a circle, dropped to the ground and curled into a ball.

Kara chuckled. "These guys are wearing her out."

The other four puppies, encouraged by Snowball's bravery, crept into the corridor separating the two rows of enclosures. Curious about their new surroundings, they sniffed and explored, bumping into each other in their excitement.

Shane crossed his arms over his chest. "This is just what the doctor ordered."

"How are things going?"

News of Finn's death had inspired a curious mix of re-actions in the resort guests. She'd caught snippets of conversation in the dining room. They were mostly treating Finn's death combined with Walt's murder as a chance for amateur sleuthing rather than a source of danger. Since no one at the resort seemed to know either of the men, no one seemed particularly worried that they were in danger.

"Things are quiet at the hotel," Shane said. "It's a lot easier to keep track of people when they go to bed. Thankfully, most of the guests here consider eight o'clock bedtime."

He stifled a yawn behind his fisted hand.

She patted Noelle's downy fur, one of two females in the litter. "Finn asked if you were trustworthy. I keep circling back to that. Do you think he had trouble with law enforcement before?"

Her own past had made her wary. Not until this week-end had she realized how deeply her distrust ran. Or how unwarranted her feelings had become. Her life before WITSEC was a distorted jumble of emotions and memories. She'd lumped all her insecurities and fears together and had never bothered to sort them out.

Jack's death had left her feeling helpless and afraid, and she'd applied those feelings to everyone she'd made contact with during that time. She'd felt as though her life and her decisions had been snatched out of her hands. Being at the mercy of others had terrified her.

Looking back, she realized everyone had done the best they could to help her. The marshals had placed her in a state she'd grown to love and in a job helping Walt that had transformed her life for the better. When she thought of the social workers and the police who'd tried to intervene on her behalf, she'd seen them as intruders. The life she'd had with her mother, though often filled with neglect, was the life she'd known—the life she'd understood. The drugs, the neglect, the arguments had felt normal because that's all she'd ever known.

With a child's mentality, she'd often assigned the blame for the situation to herself. If she'd washed her hair better, maybe the teacher from school wouldn't have called. If she'd cleaned up her room better, maybe the social worker wouldn't be talking to her mom in hushed, urgent tones.

By refusing to revisit her past, she'd let her tangled memories overlap and fester.

"You look good in a uniform," she blurted.

This time she was certain he blushed.

"Where did that come from?" he asked.

"I don't know. I guess I was thinking about something you said before. I've never had the chance to see you work up close like this."

"That's probably good." He chuckled. "The people who see me at work are generally the ones I'm arresting."

"Knowing you're here, seeing the uniform, you make me feel safe."

"Tomorrow is going to be better. We'll have more officers. I'll make sure you're taken to a secure location until this is all over."

Noelle gnawed on her cuff, and Kara carefully disengaged the surprisingly sharp little teeth. "We have to be missing something. But what?"

"I've been asking myself the same question." One of the puppies bit Shane's bootlace and tugged. "I can't figure out how Finn's death connects to all this. There was nothing of note in the papers he left in his room. We still haven't found his phone. The consensus is that it's at the bottom of the pool. So far, we haven't come up with anything out of the ordinary. He was taking water samples. Testing them. That's it."

"Do you think he found something in the water? Something...I don't know, dangerous?"

"It seems unlikely. I grew up here. The hot springs have been studied by more than just Finn. Still, it's worth checking out. I'll contact his university and see if they have a record of his results."

"And the phone call? The one he made to me?"

"We may never know," Shane said. "Red is about the only one I trust around here, so I'm having him track Mark's movements. That's all I can do for now."

One of the puppies brought a length of rope from the kennel, and Kara playfully tugged on the end. "Walt liked to read. He read a lot of nonfiction, but he also read a lot of Westerns and books about the Old West. Zane Grey. That sort of thing. If he'd been born in another time, he'd have been a cowboy."

Walt's death was still new and raw, but talking about

him helped alleviate the pain. She was grateful that Shane seemed to understand.

"And he never married." Shane unzipped his parka, leaned forward, then shimmied out of the sleeves. "I don't know why that surprises me."

"He had plenty of opportunities, that's for sure. There were always women making moon eyes at him when we worked at Denali. He said he was set in his ways and genuinely happy. I guess he figured his life was just about perfect, and he didn't need anything else." The puppy whipped his rope into the air and trotted off after it. "I envied him that."

"For being alone?"

"For being alone without being lonely." She tugged at a loose thread on the cuff of her coat. "I was as close to him as anybody ever was. Even at that, once I went to college, we'd go weeks without talking. Sometimes months. Time didn't mean much to Walt."

"Sounds like you were still the most important person in his life. It was you he called after he moved here."

"That's true. He was a decade past retirement age already. His mom had been gone for five years before he decided to move back. To be honest, I didn't even know he owned the property until he called me out of the blue. He never talked about it."

"I knew his mom, you know. Old Mrs. Tsosie. Everyone knew her."

Kara twisted toward him. "You did? What was she like?"

Her knowledge of Walt started the day she'd arrived at Denali State Park. Now she wondered what his life had been before that. What had he been like growing up? Had he ever missed his work with the marshals? She'd never asked. Now it was too late.

Shane gazed into the distance, as though he was staring into the past. "I suppose Walt's mom was a lot like Walt. She kept to herself. Kept to her routine. She went to church every Sunday and did her shopping in town every Wednesday."

He gave a tight smile. "She drove my dad crazy. Every summer she'd hire a couple of guys from town to clear the trees and brush from the west side of her property, then she'd set up a clothesline and hang her laundry out to dry. I can hear my dad like it was yesterday. *My guests are not paying a thousand dollars a night to see someone else's skivvies flapping in the breeze.* They never missed an opportunity to goad each other."

"What started the feud, anyway? Walt never talked about it."

"Depends on who you ask, I suppose. When Alaska became a state in fifty-nine, it was still pretty much the Wild West out here." He smiled. "Walt would have liked it. Not everything was good, mind you. There was a lot going on that wasn't exactly aboveboard. The same piece of land being sold multiple times. That sort of thing. A lot of people who figured the law didn't apply to them. You had to be made of iron to survive out here."

"I can imagine."

"If you were born into the Taylor family, the story went something like this. Walt's dad and my grandfather wanted to buy the same plot of land. My grandfather came up with the money first. Out of spite, the Tsosie family bought the land between the hot springs and town. That meant the only way in or out of the resort was through the Da'nai Pass. That meant the resort was only open during the summer months. The weather has gradually been warming up here. Snowfall is less. Avalanches are fewer. About a decade ago, my dad was finally able to open the resort in the winter for northern lights viewing. That increased profits by twenty-five percent. I know, because every time I reminded him about how dangerous it was to drive that road in the winter, that's what he'd say."

While all that seemed logical and straightforward, Kara suspected there was more to the story. "And if you were born into the Tsosie family, what story did you hear then?"

"From what I can gather, Walt's dad said he'd already paid for the land. He said the Taylors had stolen it from him. No one from my family was going to admit to stealing anything, even if they had. Walt's dad even went to court and tried to sue. The bank had record of a withdrawal for a large sum of money, but no record of who'd received the payment. Bank records weren't what they're like today. The lawyer who brokered the deal claimed ignorance. Walt's dad produced correspondence indicating his offer to buy had been accepted, but with the broker denying any knowledge, there was no way to prove the papers weren't forged. Without a deed, he didn't have a case. Which meant all the Tsosie family could do was block the road and hang out their skivvies to destroy the view."

"What do you think happened?"

"I think anything is possible. All you'd need is a corrupt broker and someone at the courthouse willing to take a bribe. There's never a shortage of dishonest people."

As she considered all the possibilities, her pulse raced. "What if someone found proof that Walt's dad paid for the land? What then? You said yourself that Finn was doing research on the history of the hot springs. That sounds like something worth killing over."

Her face blanched. That would place suspicion directly on Shane's stepbrother.

"Wouldn't matter." Shane flipped up his palms. "Alaska has something called an adverse possession law. Comes up so often I've memorized the statute." He cleared his throat. *"Anyone openly possessing a parcel of property under color of title for at least seven years, or at least ten years under a good faith, but mistaken, belief that the land was already part of their property, may claim that property."*

Her excitement faded. "Well that doesn't seem fair. Doesn't that mean the law is set up to protect squatters?"

"Yes and no. It's mostly used to decide boundary disputes. Someone builds a fence and maintains it for twenty years, then someone else discovers the fence was two inches over the property line. The first party can argue adverse possession. No one disputed the fence for twenty years, ergo, adverse possession."

"Still doesn't seem fair."

"That's the law for you."

"What did you think about the feud growing up?"

"Didn't think about it much, to tell the truth. Dad sometimes ordered the plow drivers to pile extra snow at the end of Mrs. Tsosie's drive. It burned him that she used part of the road he paid to plow. I told them not to. That's pretty much it."

"That's it. You never thought about it beyond that?"

"Nope. Didn't plan on getting into the hotel business. Didn't care."

His lips thinned and the lines next to his mouth

creased when he spoke about the resort. She'd always thought he was indifferent to the business, but there was more to his reaction than indifference. Since he rarely spoke about his dad, she had to guess the bitterness led back to him. Come to think of it, he rarely spoke of his mom, either. Though the one time he'd mentioned her, he'd seemed melancholy.

One of the puppies rolled to his side to display his milk tummy. She obliged by giving him a friendly pat. "I should have talked to Walt about the easement. I'm sorry. You were right. Safety outweighs an old grudge. Look what happened."

"The avalanche was still going to happen whether or not you spoke with him."

"I know. But I could have listened closer to what you were trying to tell me."

"I could have been more sensitive. I'm sorry about that." Snowball crawled into Shane's lap, turned three times just like he'd seen his mama do, then plopped down, his head resting on Shane's thigh. "The truth is that Graham and my dad made the choice to keep the resort open during the winter months. They knew the risk, and they did it anyway. We all got complacent because there hasn't been that much snow for a few years. Mother Nature caught up to us."

"Do you think Walt's death is the end of the feud? Graham can finally buy the property now, can't he?"

"As far as I know, the land is being donated to a wildlife trust. That's what Mrs. Tsosie always told people. I guarantee no wildlife trust is going to turn around and sell that land to a development."

"I suppose I'm grasping at straws. There's no way for the resort to benefit from Walt's death. If anything, it's made things worse for your stepbrother, hasn't it? When Walt was alive, at least Graham had a chance."

"Looks like it. Doesn't mean we shouldn't consider all the possible motivations. The feud is an obvious place to look."

He was humoring her. He'd obviously gone through all the possibilities already. Everything circled back to her. Walt's murder. The postcard from Florida. Finn was the only piece of the puzzle that didn't quite fit.

The puppies had tired of their play and wandered back into the kennel to nestle against Zoya for the night. All but Snowball, who opened one eye as his siblings passed by, then closed it again and burrowed deeper into Shane's warmth.

For the first time, she discovered she was frustrated with Shane's dispassionate answers. She'd always prided herself on not being nosy. She gave people their space. Even Walt. With Shane, that wasn't good enough.

He gave her the facts, but he never told her how he *felt* about anything. He was friendly and nice. He was caring. When she really thought about it, she didn't know how he felt about anything—let alone how he felt about *her*. He never sidestepped or deflected her questions, yet the answers he provided rarely gave her insight. He gave the illusion of being open without any substance.

This should have been the perfect relationship for her. In the past, she'd felt smothered by people who shared too much or got too close. The people whose attention and affection she coveted most, those she had the strongest feelings for, were the most unavailable and unattainable. She'd been closer to Walt than anyone in her life. Even her mom. Even Jack.

If she really looked closely at their relationship, Walt

had been safe. Because he was the only one who knew about her past, they'd had an automatic connection. They'd never delved any deeper. She knew the name of every favorite sled dog he'd owned in his life, but she hadn't known he was raised in Kodiak Springs until he called her six months ago. She knew his favorite Zane Grey novel was *Riders of the Purple Sage*, but she didn't know if he'd ever considered having kids. She knew he went for prime rib every Thursday night at the restaurant in town, but she didn't know his family planned on donating his property to a wildlife preserve. They'd never talked about stuff like that.

There'd been nothing wrong with her relationship with Walt—nothing she'd change even if it wasn't too late. She simply craved something different. Something *more*.

Was that what people felt about *her*? The friendships she'd had over the years had been mostly superficial. When they got together, she'd hovered around the fringes. People often accused her of putting up barriers, of not letting them get close to her. She'd never really understood how that must feel until now.

With a jolt, everything fell into place. No wonder she'd wound up with Shane, even if it had only been for a short time. They were both looking for the safe choice. They were both looking for the easy way out. The minute there'd been the slightest friction between them, they'd both bailed.

Sure, she'd told herself it was because he wanted too much information, and that was true, as well. There were other things at play, though. Other forces pushing on her that she was only just recognizing. In order to address them, she'd have to change. She didn't know if she could.

She glanced at Snowball and sighed. Animals had an

instinct for people. They saw through subterfuge and right to the heart. Because they weren't distracted by language and words; they were attuned to people's actions.

She knew one thing for certain—for any relationship to work, both people had to be invested. If she wanted to have a better relationship with Shane, she was going to have to be vulnerable. She was going to have to change.

Shane's breathing had grown deep and even. He'd fallen asleep. She'd never seen him this relaxed before. She gazed at his sleeping face. Even if she loved him enough to change herself, was it possible for him to love her enough to meet her halfway?

None of that mattered, anyway. She was leaving soon. For good. She'd start over in a new town with a new name. Whatever might have happened, it was too late now.

ELEVEN

The sound of whirring helicopter blades was the most beautiful sound Shane had heard in a month of Sundays.

The sun had risen that morning to reveal bright and clear skies. With the fresh blanket of snow, everything was crisp and fresh and new. The windswept drifts came to razor-sharp points.

The short days meant they had to work quickly before nightfall descended once more. They'd cleared a space in the overflow parking lot at the edge of the property for the helicopter to land. The moment the skids touched down, three men exited the belly. Bent at the waist with their heads down, they jogged to where Shane was standing beside a borrowed SUV.

When they'd cleared the safe distance, one of the officers stuck out his hand. "I'm Captain Banks from the ABI. This is Fritz and Miller. I heard you've been busy up here."

Shane liked him immediately. "Yep."

Banks wasn't quite as fit as the other two men, and his nose was bulbous at the end, making him look as though he was a caricature.

The four men scrambled inside the SUV. Even with

the clear, sunny skies, the temperature was still below freezing.

They drove the short distance to the resort, and Shane led the men inside.

"I've got a conference room set up for you," he said. "Any updates on the road?"

"Now that the weather has cleared, we should have the road plowed by this afternoon," Banks replied. "We'll be able to move trucks in and out as soon as that's done. We were able to clear the road as far as Mr. Tsosie's already."

"And the guests?"

"Your safety officer is sending additional troopers in on snow machines. They'll take statements and begin preparing for the evacuation once the road is clear. With two murders and no one in custody, we can't risk anyone staying. Not to mention, now that they know there's been a second murder, I doubt anyone wants to stay. That's about all we can do for now. Unless more evidence comes to light, we can't hold anybody."

"And the deceased? The geologist?"

"We'll fly him out first thing. He'll be transferred to the medical examiner in Anchorage. The helo will return for my team. You said there's a witness to Mr. Tsosie's shooting?"

"She was there at the time of the shooting, but she didn't see the perpetrator. I'd like to fly her out with you guys. The threat to her is credible."

"I'll see what I can do. I need her back at the scene to map out the shots. Since we managed to get the road cleared as far as Mr. Tsosie's house late yesterday, we have some initial findings. The coroner isn't confident the bullet will be viable for ballistics. The team wasn't able to search for any additional discharged bullets because they ran out of daylight. If I can get your witness up there, I'll have a better chance tracing the shots."

The idea of taking Kara back to the scene made Shane uneasy. "I'll speak with her."

"How's our access?"

"Not good," he said, picturing the route to Walt's. "You won't be able to get an ATV through the avalanche areas, but snow machines are an option."

"What about cross-country? I looked at the terrain from the aerial. It's less than a quarter of the distance as the crow flies."

"It's possible." There weren't many people in Kodiak Springs able to navigate the trail in these conditions. "The witness knows the trails better than anyone."

"All right. We'll get an ETA on the team coming from town. I don't want to wait on them. We're burning daylight and I want all the time I can get to search for evidence. I'll need you with me, as well. You're the most familiar with the events."

"That means we'll be leaving resort security in charge."

Banks considered the problem. "All right. I'll leave Fritz. The troopers Jeff is sending are only about an hour behind us. You've been alone for two days—Fritz should be all right for an hour."

"I'll hook him up with resort security. Tell him to keep an eye on the manager, Mark. I'll point him out. He's a person of interest."

"This is the plan," Banks said. "We'll need about an hour of prep. Get us some transportation and we'll do a sweep for evidence. Forensics will be able to reach the house from the highway. Keep the shelter-in-place order on the guests until all the interviews are conducted."

"Will do."

"We'll need to interview the employees, as well."

"It's arranged."

"Good. Let me know when you've got our transportation sorted out." The captain started toward the lounge with his team close on his heels. When he reached the door, he pivoted. "Good work, sergeant. Not the kind of thing they see in the lower forty-eight. Alaska tests a man."

Shane lifted his chin in acknowledgement. "That it does."

He turned toward the front desk. For the first time since Walt's death, he felt a spark of optimism. The weather had cleared, and he finally had backup. Until he knew the identity of the killer, delivering Finn's body to the coroner and collecting evidence was paramount.

The only hitch in the plan was evacuating the guests. If the interviews didn't reveal any obvious suspects, they'd have to release them. Once people scattered, the logistics of bringing them back to Alaska to face a possible trial became complicated.

He tapped on Kara's door.

She greeted him with a smile that took him aback for a second. Until that moment, he hadn't realized how much he'd missed her smile. Everything else was the same. She was wearing the same sweater and jeans the hotel had been laundering each evening. Her hair was pulled back into the same long ponytail, and her eyes were the same warm butterscotch.

The delicate lines of fatigue feathering from the corners of her eyes highlighted her fragile appearance. His mouth went dry and his heart thumped in his chest.

When she caught him staring, she plucked at her

sweater. "I'm going to throw this thing away when I get home. You must be as sick of looking at it as I am."

"Right back at you." He ran his hand down the front of his uniform. "I haven't been out of this thing in forty-eight hours."

She tweaked his badge. "I like it."

Something had shifted between them. He'd noticed the change when they were sitting with the puppies. He'd thought the difference was an anomaly. A litter of sleepy puppies had a way of mellowing even the toughest people.

Her smile was soft and open, and there wasn't a hint of the tension she usually carried with her when he was in uniform. He'd thought she was joking, but maybe she actually liked how he looked.

Suddenly forty-eight hours in the same outfit didn't seem quite so bad.

"Come in." She stepped aside and made a sweeping motion with her arm. "Looks like this will be my last round of room service. I figured I might as well enjoy it."

She picked up a carafe and held a coffee cup aloft with her other hand. "Like some?"

"Sure. But only a quick one."

She didn't ask if he needed sugar or cream, and his heart did another rat-a-tat-tat in his chest. He'd never appreciated the casual familiarity of knowing someone well until now. He'd never stayed with anyone long enough to reach the stage where they spoke in shorthand. As he watched her add cream to her own cup, he realized that he'd learned more about her in the past two days than he had in all the time they'd dated.

She was finally opening up to him, the one thing he'd wanted all along. Had it come too late?

"We'll all be getting out of here soon, right?" She

spoke over the brim of her cup. "Graham said the road should be cleared by this afternoon."

"That's the plan. Even if they run into trouble, we'll be out by tomorrow."

"Don't get me wrong, this place is nicer than my house and the food is top-notch, but I'm ready for my lumpy couch and dinner from a can."

He couldn't help but laugh. "You and me both."

"You think we can visit the dogs again before then?"

"About that." His good humor fled. "The helicopter just brought in the team from ABI."

"What's ABI?"

"Alaska Bureau of Investigations. They want to see if they can get ballistics on one of the bullets from Walt's house." He didn't mention that the slug in Walt had been too damaged for a good identification. "They want you on scene."

Her face drained of color and she lowered her coffee cup to the table. "When?"

"Now. They're still plowing the road, and we don't have much daylight to work with."

"You want to take the shortcut, don't you?"

He thought he saw her fingers tremble before she clenched her hands. "We don't have to. If we follow the road, it'll only take us another half an hour by snow machine."

"More like forty minutes. And that's each direction. The trail is the best choice."

He'd gone and blown it with her again. He hadn't considered how taking the trail might make her feel. The last time she'd visited Walt's had been the day of his murder. Had he lost any ground he'd gained with her?

He hitched his thumbs into his security belt. "I shouldn't—"

"It's not a big deal. Don't worry about it."

She leaned forward to straighten some papers on the table and bumped her coffee cup with her elbow, splashing liquid over the surface. As she reached for some napkins, her hands visibly shook.

"I should get a towel," she said, her voice pinched.

She stood and nearly collided with him in her haste. He took the wad of napkins from her clenched fingers and dropped them over the mess. Her arms circled his waist and she pressed her cheek against his beating heart.

He put his arms around her and rested his chin on the top of her head. "It's going to be all right. Maybe not today. But someday."

"I know." She sniffled, the sound muffled against his shirt.

Away from the resort and with a police escort was probably the safest place she could be right now. The thought didn't comfort him as much as he'd hoped it would.

He set her away from him but kept his hands loosely draped on her shoulders. "The sooner we get this over with, the better. The sooner we get back to some semblance of normal, the better."

The pressure in his chest had alleviated now that he knew there was help coming from town.

"What is normal? I don't even know anymore." She glanced up at him. There were little pools in the corners of her eyes. "I thought I could handle anything by learning to manipulate my own mind. When it's cold and snowy and it doesn't seem as though the sun will shine in the sky, I read books about the desert. After I treat an abused animal, I watch something uplifting on TV. I thought I was good at coping. I don't think that anymore."

He cupped her face and ran the pad of his thumb along the delicate skin on the apple of her cheek. "Everyone has a breaking point."

"Even you?"

"Even me."

"Tell me?"

"It's not a happy story."

"I don't expect you to always tell me happy stories."

He dropped his hands and crossed to the window, staring into a day that was bright enough to make his eyes burn. "My first year working in Kodiak Springs, I executed a wellness check on my buddy's mom. I found her slumped behind the wheel of her car in a tightly closed garage. She'd dressed in her best outfit before starting the engine. I went home that night and decided I was never going back. The job wasn't for me."

"Something must have changed your mind."

"I ran into someone I'd arrested in the grocery store. She actually thanked me. Something I'd said to her had resonated. That's when I realized that nothing given from the heart is ever truly gone. A smile, a reassuring word or sympathetic ear can bring someone back to the surface. I can't save everybody, but I can save somebody. That's what keeps me going."

He'd never told anyone that story. He felt lighter, as though a weight had been lifted from him. He'd thought he was healed, but there'd been a part of him that was still carrying the burden of that awful day. He turned away from the window, and flashbulb spots from the sun crowded his vision.

"This community is fortunate to have you," Kara said.

She crossed to the double doors closing off the bedroom and paused with her hand on the knob. "I know you'll find out who did this. I've never doubted that."

She slipped behind the door before he had a chance to reply. She had more faith in him than he had in himself these days. Nothing made sense. Nothing fit. One thought kept grinding through his head. They'd been here for two days. Someone had killed Finn in that time. They had to have seen the person. There was no other way. No one was hiding in the outbuildings.

The killer was staying in the resort, Shane was certain of it. They'd probably passed each other in the corridor and sat near each other in the dining room. While he'd done his best to protect Kara, there'd always been a weakness in his defense because he was spread too thin.

The grinding thought forced its way to the surface once more.

If someone wanted to kill Kara, why wasn't she dead yet?

An hour later, Kara followed Shane to the lobby, where he stopped to speak with Mark.

The arrival of the three men from ABI had changed the mood of the resort. With news that additional law enforcement was being sent in from town, the gravity of the situation was settling over the guests like a dark cloud.

A relentless tension had taken hold of everyone, as though the resort had become a runaway train and they were barreling toward some inevitable tragedy.

Graham and Mark had gone hoarse from reassuring panicked guests that everything was under control. One of the more vocal guests was incensed that the helicopter had taken off without any additional passengers. He seemed to have one particular guest in mind: himself.

Kara borrowed some duct tape from the front desk and repaired the hole in her snow pants. She'd need her warmest gear today. She dug a hat and a pair of gloves from the lost-and-found box. A scarf might have been nice, but the box had given up all it had to offer.

When she joined Shane outside the shed where the snow machines were kept, he was speaking to two men. She used the time to search out a suitable helmet.

When Shane caught sight of her, he waved her over. "This is Dr. Kara Riley. Kara, this is Captain Banks and Sergeant Miller from the ABI."

The captain gripped her gloved with a single firm pump. "Sergeant Miller and I need you to take us through what happened the morning Mr. Tsosie was shot. The more evidence we're able to locate, the quicker we can arrest someone."

She liked Captain Banks immediately. He was a clean-shaven, burly man in his fifties with a full head of gray hair and eyes that didn't miss a detail. She'd been talked down to enough in her lifetime to appreciate when someone treated her as an equal.

"I'll do my best," she said.

Everything had happened so quickly that morning, she hoped she'd be able to remember enough details to help them.

The captain tugged his gloves over his wrists. "I hear you know these trails like the back of your hand."

"Better," she replied confidently.

The backcountry trail was one of her favorites, and not simply because it led to Walt's. The terrain was challenging but not impossible, and the view as she wove in and out of the tall pine trees was spectacular.

"Excellent," the captain said. "That's what I was hoping for. We'll follow your lead."

She looked over the three men with a critical eye. They'd all dressed adequately for the cold. A good start.

The chill was already stinging her cheeks, and she stomped her feet to keep the blood moving. "There's a foot of snow on the trail and it's not well marked. It's a tough sled ride through two narrow canyons. Stay in my tracks. Digging someone out only wastes time."

"I'll ride with Kara," Shane said. "Once we reach the clearing around the house, we'll drop back and let you guys take point."

"All right," Captain Banks said, turning to Sergeant Miller. "Even though the storm has wiped out any visible tracks, I want minimal contamination of the scene. Single file on sight. You have the metal detector?"

"Already loaded on the snow machine."

"Good. Let's get moving. The sooner we get there, the sooner we can turn this around. Clear enough?"

Everyone nodded their agreement. The three snow machines were lined up and ready to go. Kara dropped her visor into place and swung her leg over the seat of one. For an instant she flashed back to her escape from Walt's. The emotions hit her as though she was reliving the scene: grief and terror spiked with adrenaline.

Had she missed something in her frantic escape? Would walking through what happened knock loose the memory of an important detail?

Shane's weight settled behind her. "Ready?"

She set her jaw. "Ready."

Shane was a good passenger. His hands loosely

clasped her waist to keep his balance without dragging her backward. He understood when to lean into the turns and when to shift his weight forward on the steep inclines. His size made him a decent windbreak, as well.

Her skis floated along the powder and kicked up a fine spray in her wake. The fresh air felt good after being cooped up in the hotel for so long. She ignored the ache in her leg from bracing her foot. It was a small price to pay.

She glanced behind her to find the two officers were following instructions and keeping to her tracks. They were both experienced riders. The wind bit into her cheeks and her eyes watered behind her protective visor.

At the crest of the hill, she slowed. The two officers pulled beside her. Kara peeled off her helmet and pointed.

Flanked by a crescent of mountains, the Da'nai Valley stretched out before them. Eons ago, a glacier had carved its relentless path, hollowing out steps and benches in the mountainside. The resort was visible in the bowl of the valley, a scar on the otherwise pristine landscape. Barely visible in the distance, a slight shadow marked where the service road wound through the valley.

The four of them took a moment to admire the stunning view. There were times when she grew complacent about the scenery. The past few days had reminded her to treasure the beauty of God's bounty. The scenery was like an unexpected burst of joy filling her heart. Alaska was both brutal and rewarding.

Without speaking, she replaced her visor and revved the throttle. The tall pines gave way to the small clearing surrounding Walt's house. She pulled to a stop beside the snow machine she'd overturned two days ago.

Shane stood first. He inspected the crash and shook his head. "You've snapped a ski. It'll have to be towed."

Walt's house and the kennels were visible through the tangle of scraggly pine branches. There wasn't much of a clearing around the two buildings.

Captain Banks retrieved a pair of binoculars from his saddle bag and scanned the area. "I don't see anything. No recent tracks from a vehicle. No footprints. Doesn't look like anyone has been here since the day of the shooting. That's good. You never know who's listening to the police scanner. The last thing we need is a bunch of lookie-loos tearing up the place."

He traded out the binoculars for a bag of gear and Sergeant Miller did the same. The two of them donned their snowshoes.

"Hang back and try to stay warm," the captain said, his head bent as he adjusted one snowshoe. "I'll signal you when we've secured the perimeter. I want to make sure no critters, animal or otherwise, have decided to take up residence. I'll take a few pictures, then we're clear to break out the metal detector and see what we can find."

The two men marched single file toward the house.

Kara curled her toes deeper into her boots, then pulled her hat tighter around her head. Shane stomped his feet and slapped his hands.

"You okay?" Shane asked.

"It's strange, but I'm almost relieved. I don't have to dread going back for the first time anymore."

"There are going to be a lot of firsts for you this year. Some of those firsts are going to be harder than others. When things get tough, you can always talk to me, you know?"

"I know."

He focused his attention on the officers, giving her a chance to study his profile. She'd started to build a bridge over the chasm between them—a path to the friendship they'd shared before. The more time they spent together, the more she realized that Shane was building a bridge, as well. He'd never confided anything as personal as what he'd told her earlier.

She felt as though they were each revealing pieces of themselves, then scurrying back to safety. What a pair they made. They were so different, yet in a lot of ways, they were too much alike.

Without Walt, there was nothing tethering her to Kodiak Springs. Her practice was doing well, but veterinarians were in demand in lots of other small towns. There was Homer. Located on the Sterling Highway at the southern end of the Kenai Peninsula, there were epic views of both the mountains and the sea. The last time she'd visited, she'd ordered crab legs in one of the restaurants on Homer Spit. She'd watched as the fishermen brought in the catch of the day.

But when she tried to think of what her life might be like without Shane, the picture grew blank. She'd have to leave. There was no other way. Now that her cover was blown, Kodiak Springs was no longer safe. There was no way to make the relationship work, but they could at least part on a good note.

Wearing snowshoes the officers made slow progress toward the house, each of them searching for any sign of a disturbance that might give them a better picture of what had happened two days ago. They'd only been able to retrieve the body before nightfall.

Everything was peaceful today. There was no sign of the violence. The wind whistled softly through the pines and the branches popped and creaked. The mountain breeze had a crisp, fresh scent that no air freshener could ever capture.

Kara inhaled deeply and watched for the officer's signal to join them. The captain was in the lead, and something caught his attention on the way to the house. He knelt in the snow and the sergeant peered over his shoulder.

Kara exchanged a questioning glance with Shane, who shrugged. There was no way to tell what they were looking at from this distance.

The next instant, the sergeant bolted upright, yanking the captain to his feet. The two men backtracked across the clearing. His hands waving frantically in the air, the sergeant shouted something that was lost on the wind as his cumbersome snowshoes slowed his frantic retreat. The captain tripped and went down.

Kara started toward him.

She'd barely taken a step before Shane planted his hand in the middle of her chest and shoved her hard. The backs of her legs hit the snow machine and she tumbled over the seat into the soft pillow of snow. Temporarily stunned, she stared at the sky.

A pop sounded, and the next instant, the world exploded around her.

TWELVE

The ground shook beneath Kara with the force of the blast. For a moment she was paralyzed—uncertain what had just happened. Her ears rang, and she stared into the sky. Bits of fire floated to the ground. As suddenly as the world had gone blank, everything came back into sharp focus.

She reached for her snow machine and dragged herself upright. Where Walt's house had once stood, flames licked what was left of the devastated shell. Smoking debris was strewn across the clearing. Some of the larger pieces of wood were on fire. The heat melted the snow in wide, charred circles. Thick black smoke billowed in a mushroom cloud toward the sky.

Shimmering heat waves blurred her vision. Somewhere in the distance she heard a shout. The sound shook her out of her haze. Where was Shane? He'd pushed her back. He must be near.

With her nerves tightening to form one cohesive ball of fear, she willed her leg muscles to hold her upright. Her limbs felt as though they were operating separately from each other. By sheer force of will, she placed one foot in front of the other and made staggering progress toward the engulfed house.

Ash swirled like snowflakes on a breeze and caught in her hair. Heat rolled over her in waves. The acrid stench of smoke coated the back of her throat. She held her bent arm before her face and searched for the three men.

She discovered Shane first. He'd rolled to his side and was pushing himself into a standing position. She tucked her body beneath his arm, hoisting him upright, then teetered beneath his weight.

He leaned heavily on her. Half of his face was a brilliant shade of red, as though he'd gotten a sunburn on one side. The whiskers of his beard were black and curled at the ends. One eyebrow was singed and patchy. He steadied himself and pressed the heel of his hand against his ear.

"Are you all right?" she shouted.

He shook his head, then pointed at his ear and hollered, "I can't hear you."

She managed to wrestle him to one of the snow machines and he lowered himself onto the seat. His pupils looked good and a quick pat-down failed to reveal any further injuries. After a few moments, he shook his head, then blinked his eyes in an exaggerated movement.

His gaze landed on her and his eyes came into focus. "Are you all right?"

She winced at his volume.

He lurched upright and stumbled into her.

She braced him.

He placed his hands on her shoulders. "I smelled propane. That's why I pushed you."

His quick thinking had saved her from injury.

Though he wasn't quite himself, he seemed to be coming around.

"I'm okay," she shouted. "We have to check on the others."

She tugged on his sleeve and pointed to the last place she'd seen the two men. His legs unsteady, Shane immediately staggered in the direction of the officers. She fanned out a bit from his path to cover more ground.

Kara maneuvered around the burning debris and through plumes of smoke. She lifted her collar over her nose. Disoriented, she nearly tripped over Sergeant Miller.

The force of the blast had driven him deep into the snow. His face was peppered with blood from flying debris. She dropped beside him.

A quick check of his limbs showed no obvious abrasions or broken bones. There were jagged holes in his snowsuit where burning embers had melted the fabric. His eyes were closed but his heartbeat was even, and his chest moved up and down with his breathing.

She patted his cheek. "Sergeant Miller. C'mon, Sergeant. Open your eyes." After another few tries, his eyelids fluttered up. His gaze wavered, and she snapped her fingers. "Talk to me, Sergeant. Do you know where you are?"

"Blasted into a snowdrift."

"Close enough."

"Propane." He coughed, then winced. "The captain smelled propane. We were falling back when the house blew. There were fresh tracks near the house. This had to be a setup."

Relieved he was talking, she sat back on her heels. "Are you hurt anywhere else?"

"I'm hurt everywhere," he said, choking on his words. "Give me a second."

She brushed the snow from around his head, but it was hopeless. He might as well be lying on an ice block. If she didn't get him someplace warm, she feared he'd go into shock then hypothermia.

"Listen to me, Sergeant. I'm going to get help." She offered what she hoped was an encouraging grin. "Don't go anywhere, all right?"

He gestured toward his hip. "My radio. We're still in range."

She pulled the radio from its holder and pressed the button. "We need help here. We've got two men down." They'd have heard the explosion. She tucked his arms onto his chest. "Keep your hands in tight. It will keep you warmer."

The fire had jumped to the wood structure of the kennel. Embers danced and smoked over the roof. Kara discovered Shane searching through the larger pieces of smoking debris.

"I can't find the captain," he shouted.

The fire crackled and popped around them.

She gestured in the hopes that if he didn't hear her words, he'd at least recognize her intention. "I'll check this side."

Kara thought back to the moment before the blast. The sergeant had been in the lead and the captain had just fallen. She judged the spot where the other officer had landed and gauged where the captain might have gone down.

As she neared the house, the flames grew hotter and she held her forearm before her face once more. She wasn't going from the frying pan to the fire, she was going from the fire to the freezer. The sharp fluctuations in temperature were disconcerting.

The debris got larger the closer she inched toward the house. There were chunks the size of garage doors splintered in the snow.

She discovered the captain's snowshoe first, half buried. She rushed over. He was partially covered by the back door. As she struggled to lift the edge, Shane appeared beside her and easily tossed the heavy door to one side.

The captain hissed at the sudden release. His left arm and right leg were at odd angles. They were broken, though no blood was seeping through his clothing. That meant they probably weren't compound fractures. Probably.

She slipped off her hat and pressed the material against a gash in his forehead, then checked his pupils, relieved to find they were equally dilated.

A rumbling sound lifted her gaze toward the sky. A helicopter hovered overhead. The pilot veered, circling around the billowing smoke.

Shane covered her hand to hold the makeshift bandage in place. "Flag him down!"

Kara stood and waved her arms to mark their position.

Chatter sounded from the two-way radio and she fumbled to locate the call button. "We need help here. We've got two men down."

"Ten four. No adequate landing area. Can you evacuate them on sleds?"

She considered both men's injuries. "Maybe one, but not the other. He's got multiple broken bones and a possible concussion."

"Contacting the Coast Guard out of Kodiak for an air evacuation."

As the helicopter lifted, the blades forced the smoke into a downdraft, and a black cloud enveloped her. Shane dove over the captain to protect him. Her eyes watered and she ducked her head.

When the smoke cleared, she turned to Shane. "Did you hear that? They're sending a Coast Guard helicopter out of Kodiak. Their teams have the ability to airlift. How long does that take?"

"An hour, maybe. Longer if the medic isn't on-site."

She gestured toward Miller. "I don't think he's got any broken bones, and he isn't showing any signs of a concussion. We need to keep him warm though. We need to get him out of the snow."

The irony that they were standing ten feet from an engulfed house wasn't lost on either of them.

Shane balanced unsteadily on one knee, his other leg bent. "All the snow machines have thermal blankets in the saddlebags. I'll check for a first aid kit."

"I'll see if I can stabilize his injuries."

People were a far cry from animals, but a lot of the basic first aid techniques held true for both species—assess, stabilize and evacuate. She needed to watch for signs of shock. In this cold weather, an hour might as well be a lifetime.

The captain groaned and his head lolled to the side.

She lifted her hat to see if the bleeding had slowed. "You're going to be all right, Captain. Help is on the way. We're going to keep talking so I can make certain you're not going into shock."

Some of the color had returned to his face though his breathing was shallow and labored.

His eyes came open, revealing the whites before his irises rolled into view. "You're a veterinarian, aren't you?"

"Yep."

"How do I look?"

"I've seen worse."

He coughed. "Good. Don't put me to sleep. I still have some good years left."

With his sense of humor intact, she figured he'd pull through just fine. "I normally have to worry about my patients biting me. If you can avoid that, I'll give you a Milk-Bone."

He chuckled, then his face contorted. "Don't make me laugh." He took a ragged breath. "How's Miller?"

"Better than you. He got the wind knocked out of him, but he doesn't appear to have any broken bones. Just some minor facial lacerations."

"You should be looking after him, not me."

"He's all right for now. I triage according to injuries, and you're first in line."

The wind shifted and a thick plume of smoke rolled over them. Kara leaned over the captain, shielding him as best she could.

Her eyes watered and her lungs burned. They needed to get him away from the worst of the smoke.

The radio she'd taken from Miller sounded and she held it to her ear.

There was static, then a voice spoke, "Assistance en route. Estimated arrival, thirty minutes."

"Are they bringing supplies? We need something to keep these guys warm."

"Ten four. Supplies are en route."

The captain's shoulders trembled. The little color he'd

regained in his face appeared to be draining once more. Unless she got him out of the snow and off the ground, she feared he'd continue to deteriorate. The thermal blankets could only do so much in this temperature. He couldn't wait another thirty minutes or more before assistance arrived.

She searched the clearing for inspiration. They needed something to use as a stretcher.

The door they'd pulled off the captain earlier was cracked down the middle. No help there. The other pieces of debris that were large enough to hold him were being devoured by flames.

The roof of the kennels was smoldering, but Walt's collapsible sled was in there. It would make a perfect stretcher. She glanced up and caught sight of Shane returning with his arms full of supplies. She doubted he'd approve of this plan.

"I'll be right back," she told the injured man. "Don't go anywhere."

"Don't worry." He offered a frail grin. "I'll be here."

She yanked her collar as high as it would go to partially cover her nose and mouth, then flipped up the hood of her coat. As she neared the flaming hulk of what was left of Walt's house, the heat scorched her exposed skin.

The kennels were in better shape, though the flames on the roof were growing taller. She peered inside and discovered the smoke was hovering near the ceiling. The last time she'd seen the sled, it was stored in the far-right corner. If she stayed low enough, she should make the distance and be out before the ceiling of smoke lowered.

Ducking her head, she pressed the door fully open and sprinted inside. The rickety door slammed behind her, plunging her into darkness. Unwilling to waste any more time, she navigated by memory, counting five steps and turning left. Counting four additional steps, she turned to her right and reached out her hand.

Something caught her hair and yanked her neck back in a painful stretch. She shrieked and groped to release her hair. Her fingers closed around a man's wrist.

Adrenaline spiked through her system and she wrenched herself free. As she whipped around, a sharp blow caught the side of her face. She stumbled backward and her foot caught on something. Unable to catch herself, she landed hard.

Though every instinct in her body screamed for her to keep moving, she went deathly still. If her attacker thought she was incapacitated, there was a chance he'd leave her to the burning building.

Her pulse thudded and her lungs burned. The fire crackled around her, drowning out any other noise.

She silently began reciting Psalm 23:2. If nothing further happened by the time she reached the end, she'd open her eyes.

Dizzy with terror, the words scrolled through her head, "I shall not fear…"

Footsteps thudded near her face. She cracked one eye and discovered she was lying next to Walt's sled. The footsteps appeared to be receding, but the smoke was choking her.

Her pulse raced. She didn't want to die. Not like this.

Shane had gathered all the thermal blankets he could find in the snow machine saddlebags along with the first aid kits, then returned to find Miller sitting up. The man's head was bent, and he braced one arm at his side.

"Steady," Shane ordered gently. "You're not out of the woods yet."

"Where's the captain?"

"He's all right. You need to worry about yourself now." Shane draped a blanket over the man's shoulders. "Sit tight. Help is on the way."

Miller started to rise.

Shane applied light pressure to his shoulder. "Stay down. I can't take proper care of the captain if I'm worried about you."

His words appeared to penetrate Miller's efforts, and he settled back. "Take care of him."

Shane glanced to where they'd discovered the captain, and his heart seized. Kara was nowhere in sight. With Walt's house collapsing in on itself, there weren't too many places she could have gone.

His gaze shot to the kennel structure. *She wouldn't.*

Who was he kidding? Of course, she would.

Stopping only to hastily cover the captain with the remaining two blankets, he jogged the distance and ducked inside the flaming building. When the door slammed shut behind him, he spun around and kicked it open, then scuffed in the dirt until he discovered a large rock.

He propped open the door with it and returned inside.

Smoke billowed above him, and he crouched. The crackling fire echoed through the space. He staggered forward with his arms outstretched. In his haste, he nearly tripped over Kara.

She scooted away. He reached down and she swung at him. He caught her hand. "It's me. Shane."

She pushed onto her knees and reached for something. Through his watering eyes, he managed to see that she was wrestling a collapsible dog sled toward the door. The aluminum frame was more awkward to carry than heavy.

He circled her upper arm with his hand. "We gotta get out of here. It's not safe."

She shook free of his hold. "Grab the other end."

"Fine."

There was no point in wasting time arguing; the sooner they were out of there the better. He easily lifted the sled and backed toward the door. He could carry it by himself, but he wanted a tether to Kara. The smoke ceiling had lowered in seconds. Picking up speed, he practically dragged Kara along. He held his breath until they were outside once more.

Kara dropped her end of the sled and did a frantic jig.

When she turned, he spotted flames devouring the hem of her coat. He caught hold of her and wrapped her in a tight bear-hug, dragging them both into the snow. He anxiously patted her down, then scooped handfuls of snow and continued dousing the flames.

"It's out. I'm all right." She caught his hands.

Her words took a moment to register.

"It's all right," she said again, her voice softer.

He slouched back. "Are you sure? Are you burned?"

"No." She sprang to her feet and brushed at her legs. "I'm fine. It just got my coat."

His gaze narrowed. "You're hurt. Your face?"

"There was someone in there. He knocked me down and I pretended to be dead."

His gut twisted. "We have to—"

She shook her head. "If he wants to kill me, he has to come out of the shadows. I'm not going down cowering."

He wanted to shout in rage. Instead, he radioed the

helicopter and asked them to search for any sign of the man who'd assaulted Kara.

"Are you sure you're all right?"

"Positive."

Despite the bruising, she appeared otherwise unharmed. If he didn't at least try to find the killer, she might suffer a worse fate.

"Take care of the captain," he said. "I'll be back."

He circled around the building and discovered a set of tracks leading away. Melting snow fell from the tree limbs and he followed the tracks. His feet slipped along the trail and he skidded to a halt near a steep ridge.

The evergreens were dense, and the fire was loud enough to drown out most sounds. He scuffed along the trail and discovered a set of snow machine tracks leading away.

"No!" he shouted, knowing there was no one to hear his frustration.

He radioed the helicopter once more. "He's on a snow machine. The tracks lead toward the road. Can you see him?"

"We can't see anything. The smoke is too heavy. We've had to back away. We'll open the circle and see what we can see."

Shane stood a moment in indecision. There was no way he was going to catch up. There were injured officers, and if the killer was running, he wasn't a threat.

When he arrived back at the scene of the burning house, he discovered Miller and Kara leaning over the captain. Shane breathed a sigh of relief. As long as Miller was upright and moving around, he must be doing better. He appeared to be mostly recovered, save for a buckshot pattern of abrasions on his face.

Kara knelt beside the captain, then lifted her gaze to them. "I need two lengths of wood to use as splints for his legs and two shorter sections for his arm." She held her palms apart to show the size. "All right?"

Appearing grateful to have a purpose, Miller pivoted on his heel.

"Check the first aid kit for bandages." She addressed Shane. "I need something to tie the splints."

Since he'd already started to assemble the items she needed, he went to the pile of supplies he'd dropped and made quick work of the job. When he returned, Kara was kneeling over the captain's injured leg.

She stuck out her hand. "I need scissors and bandages."

Rummaging through the first aid kit, he quickly discovered what she needed. She began unfurling a roll of bandages and cutting them into strips. By the time she'd finished, Miller had returned with the splints.

She placed one on either side of the captain's leg, being careful not to jostle him.

Shane kept one hand on his weapon in case his hunch was wrong and the killer returned. Until they caught this guy, he wasn't letting down his guard.

The helicopter was keeping an eye out for them, as well.

Kara rested a hand on the captain's shoulder. "All right. You think we're on a first name basis now? I'm Kara."

"Gabe."

"All right, Gabe. Here's what's going to happen. We're going to splint your leg. I'll stabilize the injury while we secure the splints with the bandages. That way, we move you as little as possible. We'll do the same with your arm. When that's all done, the three of us are going to carefully transfer you to this sled to keep you out of the snow. Sound good?"

Shane admired her focus.

"You're the boss," the captain said.

She grinned. "That's right. We're keeping tabs on the Coast Guard helicopter. You get to be the first one they rescue."

Straining his neck, Gabe searched out his sergeant. "What about him?"

"He's going to help splint your leg, then he'll ride back to the resort the way he came. He's tough. He'll be fine."

The captain didn't appear happy about these instructions, but his strength was giving out and he collapsed back once more.

True to her word, Kara was efficient and scrupulously careful as they braced the man's leg between the two splints. Under the guise of explaining to the captain what was happening, she meticulously talked them through each step.

She spoke gently and confidently as they worked. Even as the fire raged behind them, the three men hung on her every word. Before any of them were fully aware, Kara's quiet assurance had placed her firmly in charge of the scene.

The captain grimaced as she worked, his lips pulled back as the breath hissed through his teeth. His complexion was ashen, and a fine sheen of perspiration spread across his forehead.

When the splints were in place, she scooted back. "You're doing great, Gabe. When you tell this story at your retirement party, be sure and mention my heroic efforts."

The quip earned her another weak smile. "Will do."

"All right. I'm going to be completely honest with you. This is a collapsible sled, which means it flattens and it's closer to the ground. That'll make it easier when we slide you onto it. No matter how careful we are, you're going to get jostled a bit. Once you're secure, we'll cover you and get you as snug as a bug in a rug. How does that sound?"

"I like the last part."

Once again, she talked them through what they needed to do as they lifted the injured man. With Kara supporting one leg and Miller the other, Shane lifted his shoulders, and they worked as quickly and smoothly as they could. The movement caused a shout of pain.

In order to stay out of the smoke of the fire, they carefully shifted the captain beyond the circle of radiant heat. Miller handed over his thermal blanket and Kara tucked the extra covering over the captain.

The high-pitched whine of snow machines caught Shane's attention. He shaded his eyes with his hand and watched as five snow machines topped the hill. They maneuvered around the burning building and came to a stop.

Shane waded through the snow to meet them. The first rider swung his leg over the side and stood, then dragged off his helmet.

"Jeff!" Shane exclaimed. "You're a sight for sore eyes."

The remaining troopers dismounted and formed a half circle.

Jeff motioned toward the house. "What happened here? You been cooking again?"

"Someone did this on purpose. He got there first and set the trap. If the captain hadn't smelled the propane before he got to the house, we'd have two more dead bodies on our hands."

Jeff muttered. "I'm getting real sick of this guy always having the jump on us." He motioned two of the troopers forward. "These guys both have EMT training."

"Over there." Shane pointed. "That's Captain Banks and he's the worst off. Broken leg. Broken arm. Possible concussion."

One of the men retrieved a box from his snow machine while the other one left to speak with Kara.

"You'll be happy to know I've got some good news," Jeff said with a clap. "The road is cleared for one-way traffic which means we can evacuate the resort, the Coast Guard helicopter is twenty minutes out and I brought you this." He produced a thermos from the satchel at his feet. "It's coffee and it's still warm."

"Put yourself down for a raise on your next review."

"I already did."

"What about the fire?" Jeff asked.

"It'll burn itself out. Not much else around here that's going to burn in these conditions."

"All right. I'll coordinate with Alaska Fire Services. See if they can help us keep an eye on it. Just in case."

"Sounds good."

"You think he's still out there?" Jeff asked.

"Yes." Shane allowed the satisfaction to roll over him. "And he's leaving a trail that's going to lead us right to him."

THIRTEEN

"Mark?" Kara asked Shane incredulously the next day.
"You're saying the killer is Mark?"

"Looks like it," Shane replied.

They'd returned to the resort to discover a hive of activity taking place.

There were two buses parked outside the front door, and guests were gathering in the lobby with their luggage. No one appeared to be complaining. The explosion at Walt's had added an extra layer of apprehension to the group.

There were at least a dozen officers, some of them with patches that showed they worked in Anchorage. The extra authority on-site was allowing Graham to direct the guests with minimal pushback. He was operating without his right-hand man since they'd arrested Mark.

"Are you sure?" she asked.

She hadn't had a chance to speak with Shane for almost twenty-four hours. He'd been too busy with the investigation. She'd only just managed to catch up with him in the lobby when she went down for lunch.

Shane pressed the button for the second floor. "The tracks from Walt's house led directly to the resort. One of the investigators from the ABI discovered there'd been a suspicious drowning at the last hotel he managed. He quit shortly after. They decided to go over our security camera footage again. They caught him on camera, following Finn to the outdoor pool. That was enough to get a search warrant for his room. They discovered Finn's phone and computer, along with the gun they suspect killed Walt."

"But why?"

"There was a recent deposit into his bank account. The amount was significant. Looks like he was hired by someone. The information has been passed on to ABI and the marshals at WITSEC. You'll still be in protective custody until they can find out who hired him."

"And Mark won't say?"

"Not yet. Once he starts seeing the evidence piling up against him, he'll come around."

They'd reached her room and she rested her hand on the knob. "Well that explains a lot. Like how he *discovered* the postcard on the front desk. And why nothing ever showed up on the security cameras. He was probably erasing the footage as fast as they were recording. But why didn't he erase the footage of himself following Finn?"

"I don't know. Maybe he thought he had. He knew all the blind spots in the hotel. He had access to the master keys. He was perfect. Why kill Walt, though?"

"Mark knew I was going up there that morning. I always pass through the lobby on my way to the kennels. He didn't know Walt had been a marshal. If Walt caught him setting a trap for me, he wouldn't be able to talk his way out of it. Walt would have known immediately that he was lying. That's probably what they were arguing about. What I don't understand is how Finn fits into all this."

"He was always hanging out in the lobby. He must have seen something or heard something."

"Well, at least it's over now."

"Yes."

"How long do you think before the guests are cleared out?"

"Probably by this afternoon."

"I'm going to check on the dogs. They tend to sense disruption. Between the fire and the evacuation, they're probably agitated."

"Sounds good. How about I meet you in the lobby and walk you over?"

"Don't tell me you're still worried."

"Actually, I was hoping to visit with a certain puppy named Snowball."

"Well look at me flattering myself. I guess no one can compete with a puppy."

Two hours later, Kara watched the second busload of guests exit the parking lot while the employees scurried to close up the resort after them.

With everything that had happened, she was feeling oddly useless with all the activity buzzing around her. She'd promised to wait for Shane, but he'd gotten caught up in interviews with the officers and the investigators.

When she couldn't stand the confinement anymore, she donned her coat, wrinkling her nose at the smell of smoke in the material. Between that and the scorched hem, she was down another coat.

She stepped outside and glanced in the direction of Walt's house. Though the majority of the fire had burned out almost immediately, wispy tendrils of smoke drifted into the sky. If only they'd discovered that Mark was the killer an hour sooner. The captain wouldn't be in the hospital right now.

She opened the door to the kennels and began the gauntlet of greetings. Trisha peered out from the stall where Zoya and the puppies were kept.

"Hey, Doc," she called. "I'm glad you're here."

The note of concern in her voice had Kara worried. "What is it?"

"Snowball. He hasn't been acting right since the explosion. All the dogs were agitated when it happened. Everyone has calmed down except this little guy."

Trisha stepped aside to let Kara peer into the enclosure. Zoya and four of the puppies were sleeping in a haphazard pile of paws and noses. Snowball was sitting in the corner and his ears drooped.

"Poor little guy," Kara said. "I can look after him if you want to get out of here."

"Would you?" Trisha's shoulders sagged in relief. "I haven't been home in days. My mom's been feeding my cat. He's probably forgotten what I look like by now."

"Who's going to watch them over the holidays?"

"I've got that duty."

"Tell you what," Kara said. "Why don't you spend Christmas with your family, and I'll look out for these guys."

Trisha's eyes lit up. "Are you sure?"

"Positive. Go home. I'll take care of the dogs tonight."

"Thank you, thank you, thank you." Trisha pressed her palms together and nodded. "I am dying to get out of here."

Kara laughed. "Then go. I'll take care of everything."

She sat on the floor and peered at Snowball. He scooted his paws forward, then sat back up again.

When she heard the door open and close, she thought it was Trisha coming back until she heard a familiar voice call, "Hello."

She tipped her head back and leaned out of the enclosure. "Down here."

As she sat up, Snowball bounced past her. He trotted down the corridor to meet Shane.

She shook her head. "You've got a fan."

He took off his coat and hung it on a peg near the door, then scooped up the puppy. Snowball rewarded him with several enthusiastic licks.

Kara's eyes widened. "You shaved!"

He ran his hand self-consciously down his chin. "Things were a little patchy after the fire."

She wasn't certain which way she liked him best. Come to think of it, why did she have to choose? She liked him both with and without the beard.

"Have you heard from the hospital?" she asked.

"The news is good. The captain is out of surgery. Everything went well." He plopped down next to her. "You can't say it hasn't been an eventful few days."

Snowball nipped at the badge on his chest.

"I can't believe how quickly the guests cleared out."

"A murder and an explosion will do that to people."

She offered a wry grin. "Trisha said that Graham gave everyone the night off. It'll take at least another day to close up the resort. Maybe more."

"They deserve the break. They've been working non-stop for nearly three days."

"So have you." She rolled her head toward him. "Why aren't you at home?"

"Because you're here."

Her pulse tripped. "I offered to watch the dogs so Trisha could go home."

"Don't you want to go home?"

She stretched, loosening the tight muscles of her neck. "Yes. But I can keep track of the vet clinic from here just as easily as from home. Figured I might as well stay here." She hadn't meant to sound quite so pathetic. "It's all right, you know. This is what I like to do. This is where I'm happy."

Shane had ceased petting Snowball, and the puppy nudged his nose beneath Shane's hand.

"I don't know what's going to happen after this," Shane said. "And there's something I wanted to say to you in case we don't get the chance to be alone again."

She glanced at her folded hands. "What's that?"

"You were right about me," he said. "I wanted you to trust me. I wanted you to share yourself with me, but I wasn't willing to do the same. I wanted something from you that I wasn't willing to give in return."

Her heart thudded dully in her chest. "Neither of us is very good at being vulnerable."

"I don't like the resort. I don't like being here. I don't like staying here. I don't have a lot of good memories of this place." He ducked his head. "I didn't want to tell you about my family because I'm ashamed."

Her hands tightened reflexively. "I had no idea."

What did Shane have to be ashamed of?

"Most people don't. Most of the old staff from the resort are gone. My parents are gone. There's no one left to remember. No one but me. That's the problem, I guess. See, I worked my first two years in Anchorage. I'd go on calls to these houses. To these same houses. And I'd see the same things over and over and over again. I'd look at their kids and I'd see my own guilt and shame mirrored in their eyes, but I didn't figure I had a right to that kind of pain. Whenever I took someone to the battered women's shelter, I'd think how blessed I was. I grew up in paradise. I swam in the hot springs whenever I wanted. I rode my bike through the hotel. We had a second house in Texas. No matter what happened in our family, there was always food on the table. I didn't think I had a right to be anything but grateful for my life."

Her heart broke a little for him. "Oh, Shane. I'm so sorry."

The signs had been there all along. Only he was good at hiding them. Children who came from abusive homes often were.

"I grew up trying to fix things, and I always failed. Somewhere along the line I started to think I was a failure."

She reached for his hand and squeezed his fingers.

"I knew I wasn't going to be like him. I never doubted that. Instead, I just never let people get close to me. I was afraid to love someone because I was afraid of giving another person that sort of power over me again. And not just the power to hurt me, the power to make me feel helpless. I figured if I was the one to love a little less, then no one would have control over me. Does that make sense?"

"More than you'll ever know."

"You scared me, I guess. That's why I issued an ultimatum. I figured if I forced the issue, then I'd be the one in control. Turns out, that's not the way it works. I just wound up feeling like a failure again."

"You're not a failure. I didn't give you much help. I think I've always been afraid that my old life is one mistake away. I didn't want people to know about the person I was, because I feared talking about her might conjure her up again."

She'd wanted Shane to trust her, to open up to her. Now she'd have to strip away all her own lies until there was nothing left but truth, like he'd done for her. That was the only way to complete the bridge between them. All at once the challenge seemed insurmountable. The distance too far.

"We're a pair, aren't we?" he said.

"You read my mind." She smiled sadly. "As awful as these past few days have been, I'm grateful for the experience. I've always admired what you do, but I've been afraid, as well. If you were afraid to love because someone might have control over you, then I was afraid of authority for the same reason. Seeing you these past few days has been a revelation. I think I understand why you do what you do now."

The world was full of good people and bad people, and she'd known both. The trick was learning to recognize the difference. Sometimes, though, the simplest things proved to be the most complicated.

"I knew this was my calling," Shane said, his voice quietly urgent, as though he was willing her to understand. "I can't save everyone. Some days, I feel like I can't help anyone. But it's better than throwing in the towel. It's better than giving up. I can't change the world, and I can't save the world, but I can make my little corner of the world better. That's enough."

A curious numbness assailed her. He deserved so much.

"You're the bravest man I've ever known," she said.

He reddened and turned away for a moment.

"Maybe there's hope for us, after all." When he turned back, he stuck out his hand. "Friends?"

Her ears buzzed, and for a moment she felt as though she was back in the clearing when Walt's house exploded. The world shattered around her, and there was nothing left but floating embers. He was telling her goodbye. She'd known this was possible. Now that it had finally come to pass, she was almost relieved. Like all the firsts she'd go through this year after Walt's death, this was another milestone. A sad milestone, but an important one nonetheless.

She shook Shane's hand, savoring the feel of his calloused fingers one last time. "Friends."

She'd known this was coming. She'd move on. She'd start over. It wouldn't be the first time.

The stillness surrounded them, and they sat in silence. She stared ahead, trying to identify what she was feeling. She was afraid, but there was also a glimmer of hope. She'd walked a little into the fire, and she'd survived. Maybe she could go a little farther next time.

All her life she'd feared that there was something fundamentally wrong with her. There'd been this insidious feeling that she was the one at fault. That she was defective. What else explained how everything had gone so wrong in her life?

The story she'd told herself was false. There were good times and bad times in every life. Sometimes they clumped together. Other times they were spread apart. She was grateful that she'd had Walt in her life. She was grateful for all the things she'd learned from Shane.

She wasn't a person who was broken beyond repair. She was a person who learned from her mistakes.

Together she and Shane fed the dogs and cleaned out

the kennels. They worked well as a team, passing the time in quiet contemplation. Each moment felt like a gift. The future stretched out before her like a blanket of snow, clean and unblemished. Walt's death was going to hurt for a very long time, but she wasn't afraid of the pain anymore. Losing Shane was going to be hard. She'd survive.

She'd spend Christmas alone this year, but there was always the chance that next year might be different. Even while she mourned the loss of Walt and the end of her time with Shane, she knew her future was filled with possibilities, as long as she was open to them.

The work felt good and her muscles ached. They reached the end of their rows at almost the same time and smiled at the timing.

Her phone rang, and they both laughed nervously at the interruption. The area code was for a local number.

Curious, she took the call.

"Is this Dr. Riley?" a female voice asked.

"This is she."

"This is Eileen Turro."

"Walt's friend," Kara clarified.

"I guess that's what you could call me. I can't even remember a time when he wasn't in my life."

"You heard about what happened?"

"The town is all abuzz. You can't have a dozen officers descend on the town and smoke billowing into the sky without word getting out."

"I suppose not. I'm sorry." Kara's throat clogged with emotion. "I know we'll all miss him."

"He spoke fondly of you. That was a rarity for Walt. He mostly kept to himself. He held you in high regard."

Kara's eyes burned. "The feeling was returned."

"I left a message for Sergeant Taylor at the trooper

station. I haven't heard back from him. I know you two, well, uh, anyway, you hear things around town. I thought you might know where he is."

Kara blushed. "Actually, um, he's with me."

"Well I'll be. You mind if I talk to him? This involves you too."

"Why don't I put you on speakerphone?"

"All righty."

Kara held out her phone and Shane moved next to her.

"Eileen?" Kara said. "Sergeant Taylor can hear you now."

"Since I've got you both on the line, I'm starting to feel a little ridiculous. It's just that Walt asked me a legal question a few days ago, and what with everything that's happened over the past couple of days, it's been wearing on me. Probably it's just a coincidence, but it's been bothering me."

Shane leaned over the phone. "What's been bothering you, Eileen?"

"Walt hadn't been feeling well and the doctor in town sent him to Anchorage for some tests. I don't know what they told him up there, but when he got back, he asked me to change some paperwork on his estate."

Kara's chest squeezed. "But he didn't say what was wrong?"

"No. You know how he was. Getting inside that man's head was like trying to slide between two coats of paint."

"Yes," Kara said, smiling at the thought. "I know."

"Anyway, Walt wanted some advice on a rather complicated legal question involving a living trust and an original deed. It was all fairly complicated for a hypothetical question."

Kara's pulse picked up speed. "What was his question?"

"Okay. I'll try and explain it as best I can. I'm a lawyer and *I* don't understand all the bits and pieces." She heaved a sigh. "Here goes nothing. When people pass property or land to their loved ones, they generally use a trust. There are a couple different kinds, but the one Walt was asking about was specific."

"Okay. I think I follow so far."

"Say I own a piece of land and I want to put it in trust for my son. Only I don't make any provisions for what happens after my son dies. So when my son dies, the trust is closed."

"What happens to the property?"

"In the sort of trust Walt was talking about, if no provisions are made, the property reverts back to the original owner." There was another long sigh. "Now here's where it gets complicated. Walt wanted to know what would happen if two deeds were discovered, and one of them predates the other."

"That's a pretty specific hypothetical."

"That's exactly what I thought. Especially considering the rumors about what happened to Walt's father."

"What did you find out?" Kara's ears buzzed. "What would happen?"

"If there are two deeds for the same piece of property, then it means someone tried to sell the land twice. I know it sounds odd, but things like that happened before computers connected everybody. There's land in this state that was sold two and three times before the law caught up. When that happens, the person who filed the deed first is the owner. They hold the original title."

Shane and Kara exchanged a glance.

"But what if that original deed was never filed?"

"A deed doesn't have to be recorded to be a valid conveyance."

"Okay," Shane said, rubbing his forehead. "So you're saying that if a trust like Walt was talking about closed, the land would revert back to the original owner, and the original owner is the one with the oldest date on their deed?"

"That's it in a nutshell. I'm not going to lie. This doesn't come up very often."

"Couldn't someone amend the trust along the way?" Kara asked. "Before it ran out?"

"Absolutely. That's what usually happens in these cases. When the title is transferred, a good lawyer will catch the oversight and add an amendment. Unfortunately, every profession has its bad eggs."

Shane blew out a breath. "Let me get this straight. Adverse possession doesn't apply if the land is in trust."

"Exactly. Adverse possession won't apply if I give you permission to use my land. That's what the trust does. It's basically giving someone permission to use the land for a length of time. When that time is up, that time is up."

"So if you wanted to keep the land, it would be in your best interest to destroy any deeds that might dispute ownership."

"Well, it'd be illegal. But, yes, I guess. Destroying any evidence of previous ownership simplifies everything."

Nausea rose in the back of Kara's throat. "Thanks, Eileen."

Kara could almost feel Eileen shaking her head. "I had a bad feeling when I heard Walt's house had been destroyed. He had a pretty specific hypothetical question, then he gets murdered. Maybe I've been watching too many crime shows on TV, but that seemed like an awful big coincidence. That's why I wanted to speak with Shane."

Shane leaned in once more. "Have you talked to anyone else about this?"

"Nope. Just you."

"Don't talk to anyone. And I mean anyone." Shane was reaching into his pocket for his own phone. "Do you understand?"

"Don't worry about me. You don't get far in this business without knowing when to speak up and when to shut up."

Kara took the phone off speaker and held it to her ear. "Thank you, Eileen."

"Hey, before I forget, I was going to call you about another matter anyway. Walt made some provisions for you in his will. Stop by my office when you get a chance, and we can go over it."

Kara figured she was probably the proud owner of two malamutes and their five puppies. That was just the sort of thing Walt would do.

This time, she didn't mind so much. "I'll get in touch."

As she hung up the phone, the full gravity of what Eileen had just revealed struck her.

Kara lifted her anguished gaze to Shane. "It was Graham all along, wasn't it?"

FOURTEEN

Shane's knees almost buckled. They'd arrested the wrong man.

"It was him," Kara whispered. "Graham killed Walt, didn't he?"

His throat went dry. "Looks like it."

He dialed his phone. Three rings sounded before Jeff picked up.

"Was Graham on one of the buses?" he demanded without preamble.

"Hello to you too, boss."

"This is important."

"All right. Yes. I saw him by the last bus. He was accompanying a group to Anchorage to catch the charter. He told one of the troopers that he was moving up his flight to California. I guess this week was pretty hard on him."

"What time did they leave?"

"About an hour ago."

"Coordinate with the Anchorage PD and pick him up. Consider him armed and dangerous."

"We're talking about Graham, right?"

"Just do it."

"Yes, sir."

Shane hung up the phone and leaned against the wall. Kara caught his arm. "I'm so sorry."

"I was looking in the wrong place all along. This was never about you. It was always about the land."

He could practically see the wheels turning in her head.

"Why kill Finn, though? All Graham had to do was destroy the deed proving that Walt had a prior claim on the land."

"Unless Graham couldn't find the deed. Think about it. Finn finds the deed and shows it to Walt. He just thinks it's a cool piece of history, but Walt realizes the significance and tells Graham."

"Graham panics and tries to get the deed back from Walt."

"They argue. Graham shoots Walt. Only Graham can't find the deed and he's afraid it's going to turn up. The only other person who might know where it's located is Finn."

Her hands flew to her mouth. "That's why he burned Walt's house."

"Yep. After he killed Walt, he couldn't locate the deed. When Finn didn't have it, Graham decided to burn down Walt's house."

"Do you think it was there?"

"I don't care. He murdered Walt. He murdered Finn. He framed Mark. Right now, that deed is the least of my worries."

Kara paced the aisle. "Poor Mark. All the reasons we suspected him could easily be applied to Graham. He had access to the cameras. He knew the blind spots. Everything. Graham must have altered the recordings."

"I need to get to town. Do you have your keys? I'm short on transportation these days."

"They're in my room."

The two of them quickly secured the kennels and made their way back to the hotel. Twilight already darkened the sky. In another half an hour or so, it would be completely dark.

They took the shortcut through the indoor pool enclosure and crossed into the building and through the dining room. The lights were on, but the chairs had already been flipped onto the tables.

The front desk was empty.

Kara shivered and crossed her arms over her chest. With darkness falling and the resort all but deserted, an eeriness settled over her.

Shane circled around the desk. "I don't like this. Red and Pete are supposed to be here along with a half a dozen fresh staff members from town. Where are they?"

"Is there anything on the security cameras?"

"I don't see anything. Wait—"

He glanced up just as an arm wrapped around her neck. She shrieked and attempted to free herself.

Then she felt something cold press against her temple. "Don't make this any harder than it has to be." Graham spoke near her ear.

Lifting his hands above his head, Shane slowly rose to his feet. "Why don't you let her go, Graham?"

"No can do, bro." Graham's eyes had a wild, unfocused look. "This is the end of the line."

"It doesn't have to be. Let's talk this out."

"All right, let's talk." He pressed the gun tighter against Kara's temple. "Where's the deed?"

"It was at Walt's," Shane bluffed. "You burned it when you burned the house down."

"Nope. Nice try. I burned it down because I'd trashed

the place. I was worried I might leave some evidence behind. It's not there. I let the propane tank run and fired a shot from the kennel. I timed it wrong. You lived."

Kara's heart hammered against her ribs. The hotel was completely deserted. Graham must have planned this all along. He'd never arranged for the employees to come back because he'd wanted the resort empty of everyone but her. She was the only other person Walt might have left the deed with.

Shane appeared calm, but she could see the muscle tick along his jaw.

"I didn't even suspect you that first day. When you pulled up in the snowplow," Shane said tonelessly. "Finn discovered the deed, didn't he? When he was researching the hot springs."

"Can you believe it? You guys have been feuding all this time because some enterprising homesteader sold the land twice. I'd have liked to have met that fellow. Finn didn't even realize what he'd found. Walt did. He knew about the trust. I don't know how, but he did. Everyone knows everyone's business in this town."

"That's why you went to see him that morning."

"I parked the snowplow on the road. My snow machine was in the bed."

Kara sucked in a sharp breath. No matter what he said, he'd planned on killing Walt all along. Why else would he hide the snowplow on the road while he visited Walt?"

"You brought a gun," Shane said.

He'd obviously come to the same conclusion.

"A guy's gotta look out for himself. I didn't know what was going to happen."

"Walt is gone. Finn is gone. You don't need to hurt anyone else."

Shane's gaze flicked to the door and back again. "It's over. Why don't you let Kara go?"

"That's just it, though. It's not over. Walt said I'd never find the deed. I can't risk it. Once he figured out I wanted it, he knew something was up. He put it somewhere." Graham gave Kara a hard shake. "Did he give it to you?"

Shane surged forward. "Easy, there. She doesn't have it."

"How do I know that? She was the only person he ever talked to. He must have told her something."

Kara tried to jerk away but he held firm.

"How did you find out about me?" she asked. "About Florida?"

She sensed Shane was formulating a plan, and she wanted to keep Graham talking.

"Shane's computer search history. He did a pretty good job covering his tracks, but I'm better. He was stuck to you like glue after Walt died. Then he started searching a case in Florida. It was clear he thought Walt's death had something to do with you. I had a box of postcards from when I was a kid. I took a chance. It must have worked."

"And you'd let Mark go to jail for a crime he didn't commit?" she asked incredulously.

A man who was capable of murder was capable of anything.

"Collateral damage," Graham said. "I figured the best way to stop you from looking was to hand you an answer." The gun moved against her temple. "Enough talk. Put your phone, your gun and your utility belt on the counter."

Shane hesitated.

"Do it!" Graham shouted. "You too." He nudged Kara. "Give me your phone."

Shane slowly removed the items and set them on the counter.

Kara pulled out her phone and Graham snatched it, shoving it into his own pocket. "Get in the office." He pushed Kara forward. "It's easier if there are no bullets in either of you, but I'll take care of things the hard way if I need to."

"Take it easy." Shane held his ground. "You don't have to kill anyone else. We can figure this out. We grew up together. You can trust me."

"You're wrong. I've got everything wrapped up in this place. *Everything!* I spent twenty years of my life toadying up to your dad, and it finally paid off." Graham's voice shook and Kara's vision blurred around the edges. He was losing control. "Your dad wanted to stick it to you, and I gave him the opportunity. You wanna tell me why he hated you so much?"

Kara winced.

"Because I was a witness to his abuse," he said calmly. "I was a reminder of what he did. He wanted to bury the past, but he couldn't as long as I was around."

"Figured it was something like that. My mom heard rumors in town." Graham snorted. "He never really changed, did he? I'd see echoes of what he must have been like sometimes. He was a real jerk. My mom had already been married to a poor jerk. I guess she decided being married to a rich jerk was better."

Kara latched on to the mention of his mom. "Think about your mom, Graham. You don't want to do this to her."

"She'll never find out. I figure I can kill two birds with one stone. We've all been trapped here for three days, which means the deed is either here or at Walt's. If I burn this place down, I can build something better. And no one will ever know the difference."

"You can't." Shane's expression was harder than she'd ever seen before. "I won't let you."

Graham pushed Kara forward. "I—"

A gunshot sounded and Graham twisted around, his left arm flailing. As he stumbled backward, he reached out and caught Kara's ponytail, yanking her with him. Another shot rang out.

Shane dove for his gun. As he gripped the handle, he caught sight of Red falling.

Kara gripped the back of her ponytail as Graham dragged her in his wake deeper into the resort. Blood oozed from a wound on his arm, but he kept his tight grip on Kara.

Shane stalked after them. "Stop."

Graham thrust Kara before him as a shield and held the gun to her head. "Get back."

Shane stopped, his gun drawn. "It's over, Graham. Let her go."

He wouldn't take the shot with Kara between them, and Graham knew it.

"Drop your gun," Graham ordered.

"You can't shoot both of us. Why don't you aim at me—"

"No!" Kara shouted.

Graham shook her hard enough that Shane heard her teeth rattle. "Shut up."

Willing her to remain calm, Shane held her terrified gaze.

He straightened his left arm, his palm facing toward her. "It's going to be all right. Trust me, okay?"

She bit her lip and nodded.

Graham shook her again. "Where's Red?"

"You killed him."

Out of the corner of his eye, Shane could see movement from Red. Better to lie than risk having Graham finish the job.

Kara stifled a sob.

Graham dragged her backward. "Then it's just us again."

"Yep. It's just us. Why don't you let Kara go? Then it's just you and me."

"Don't pull your cop garbage on me. This isn't a negotiation. She's my insurance."

He took another halting step back.

Shane's eyes hardened. "It's too late, Graham. You've left too many bodies in your wake. You can't blame Red's death on Mark. He's in jail."

Kara's head strained to the side. Graham was maneuvering her toward the stairwell.

"You three are going to die in the fire," Graham said. His eyes had taken on a hazy, cloudy look. "It'll all be very tragic. Don't worry, I'll be very distraught about your deaths."

Graham was panicking. As long as Shane stayed calm, he had the upper hand. He had to control the situation in order to protect Kara.

"I'm giving you one more chance to let her go," he said. "Because if you hurt her, there's no place in the world you can hide from me. Do you understand?"

Graham's face turned a brilliant shade of red. He knew Shane well enough to fear the threat.

They were nearly to the exit door. As Shane watched Kara's face, he realized her mind was working. She was planning something. He met her gaze, and he felt as though she was willing him to understand. Her gaze flicked toward Graham's foot and back at him.

He nodded, indicating he understood what she was going to do.

Once she stomped on Graham's foot and ducked out of the way, he'd have a clear shot.

He kept his eyes focused on her, gauging the distance, judging when she'd make her move.

Graham glanced over his shoulder at the door. Kara nodded. She lifted her foot and stomped. As Graham howled in pain, she jerked away.

Shane fired as Graham fell against the door, pushing it open and dragging Kara with him.

He'd been so close.

He got one look at her stricken face before the door slammed shut. Shane ran the distance and pushed open the door.

Several quick shots forced him back.

Breathing like he'd just run a six-minute mile, Shane slouched against the wall. He gave himself only a few seconds before he pushed off and returned to the lobby.

Red was flat on his back near the lobby doors. He groaned and clutched the side of his head. Blood oozed from the wound.

"You all right, buddy?" Shane asked.

Red groaned. "Been better."

He shrugged out of his coat and wadded the material under Red's head, then stood and retrieved his radio from the counter. He relayed what had happened to Jeff and set the radio back down. This time there was no blizzard to slow down the ambulance and his backup. He figured he had about twenty minutes before the posse arrived.

Red's arm flopped to the side and he curled his fingers. "Go get him."

Shane nodded. "That's a promise."

He refastened his utility belt and followed the path Graham and Kara had taken. When he pushed open the door to the stairwell, the trail of blood was obvious. Maybe he hadn't missed his shot after all.

He glanced toward the lower level where the utility corridors were located. If Graham wanted to start a fire and make it look like an accident, the kitchen was the obvious place to start.

He retreated into the corridor once again, letting the door slam. Graham would be listening for him, and Shane wanted to keep him confused.

He shut off the lights in the dining room, plunging it into darkness. As he crept past the tables, he heard voices coming from the kitchen area. He fought his natural urge to rush. He needed to keep a clear head.

He hugged the wall and eased forward. The swinging door to the kitchen had never quite closed all the way, and no one had bothered to fix it over the years. Through the narrow crack, he caught sight of a hand dumping a pile of rags on the open flame of the gas stove.

Shane shoved open the door and fired.

Graham jerked back. He stumbled and collided with Kara. She fought him and Graham let out a roar, shoving her hard. She tripped backward and fell, her head striking the stainless steel worktable. Her body went limp and she collapsed to the floor.

A furious darkness descended over Shane's vision. Without considering the consequences, he dove forward. Live or die, this ended here.

Now.

FIFTEEN

Something snapped inside Shane. As he fired off another shot, he dove forward, ignoring the gun in Graham's outstretched hand. He had five inches and twenty pounds on the smaller man, and he planned to use everything he had to his advantage.

They hit the tile hard and Graham's gun skittered across the floor. Instead of going after it, Graham snatched Shane's gun hand and slammed it down. Shane's knuckles exploded in pain and his hand automatically opened.

As Shane groped for his weapon, Graham rolled to his side and kicked him in the ribs. Bones cracked and a wave of nausea swept over him. Groaning, Shane reached for the gun again. His fingers closed around the handle and he rolled onto his back.

Flames from the gas stove were licking up the side of the wall and gathering at the ceiling. Graham staggered to his feet and stood over him.

"What are you going to do?" he demanded, splaying his arms. "Are you going to shoot an unarmed man?"

"No."

"I didn't think so."

Shane heaved upward and swept his legs beneath Graham's feet. Caught off guard, Graham flipped to the side. He stretched out one arm when he landed, crushing it beneath him.

He howled in pain. "You broke my arm!"

Smoke was starting to fill the room. Shane retrieved his weapon and holstered it. Then he reached for Graham's gun, dumped out the rounds and stuck it in his waistband.

Graham clutched his arm and writhed on the floor.

Shane snatched a fire extinguisher from the wall and doused the flames, then dropped the canister and rushed to Kara's side. He cradled his hand behind her head. Blood oozed from a large goose egg.

She blinked groggily. "What happened?"

Tears flooded his eyes and he didn't try and stop them. He'd never seen a more beautiful sight. He didn't feel any of his own pain. Not the broken ribs. Not his sprained wrist. They were background noise that was easily ignored.

Graham had ceased moving and was lying on his side. His breath came in heaving gasps and his face was ashen. He was no longer a threat.

"We got him," Shane said. "We saved the day."

"I never doubted us."

Her weak smile was like sunlight streaming through a church window. He tucked her into the crook of his arm and rocked her.

She lifted her fingers to his face. "You're crying."

"I know." He choked back a sob. "I know."

"Everything is going to be all right," she said, repeating his words back to him. "Maybe not today. But someday."

"You're all right. And that's all I need. That's every-thing I need."

A cacophony of sirens sounded outside, and all the adrenaline drained from his system.

He hoisted her into his arms. As he reached the door, Graham hollered after him.

"You can't leave me here!"

His gun drawn, a state trooper burst into the kitchen.

Shane jerked his chin over his shoulder. "That's your guy. He's your problem now."

Graham wasn't much of a threat in his condition. Shane was happy to leave him behind. He was happy to leave everything behind. He never wanted to see the in-side of the resort again. Once he walked out those doors, he never planned on returning.

He emerged into the lobby as several officers came rushing through the door. His knees weakened. He took a few more halting steps before Jeff reached his side.

"He's in there." Shane jerked his chin over his shoulder. "He's broken his arm. But don't turn your back on him."

"I won't."

A paramedic was tending to Red. He couldn't feel his legs but somehow he was still moving. He wasn't stop-ping until he was through the doors.

The blue-and-red lights of the emergency vehicles danced just outside the glass. He reached the door as two firemen arrived. One of the men moved aside to let him pass.

The second fireman said something to him, but he didn't hear the words. He kept walking forward. Away from the resort. Away from the death. Away from the pain.

The fireman blocked his way. He was a big guy and Shane was running out of energy.

The man's face flooded with sympathy. "Let me take her," he said. "You're dead on your feet."

The words finally penetrated the fog swirling through Shane's brain. He let the fireman take Kara from his outstretched arms. She was safe. He could finally let go.

As soon as he released her, he dropped to his knees.

A paramedic rushed over and placed one hand on his shoulder. Shane winced. He recognized the paramedic as someone he'd gone to high school with.

"She's in good hands, Shane," the paramedic reassured him. "It's time to let us take care of you."

All the fight drained from him, leaving him weak. Maybe it was time to let someone else carry the burden. Just for a little while. Just until he got his strength back. The past few days had taken all his reserves.

He collapsed onto his back and stared at the vast blanket of stars crowding the dark sky.

He could finally rest.

Kara was contemplating the lime Jell-O on her hospital tray when a soft knock sounded on the door.

When Shane appeared, her heart jumped into her throat. He was wearing jeans and a blue-plaid buttonup shirt she recognized. He'd gotten a haircut and he'd shaved recently. She could see the slight burn of the blade on his chin. He had a duffel bag slung over one shoulder and a bouquet of flowers in his hand.

She fought the impulse to burst into tears. She'd done too much crying lately. She was ready for a little joy.

He perched on the edge of the bed and extended the hand holding the bouquet. "I brought you something."

She buried her nose in the soft petals and inhaled. "This must have cost a fortune."

"Worth every penny."

"Thank you."

"I brought you something else." He retrieved a furry little body from inside his coat. "This little guy."

Kara dropped the flowers on the tray and reached out. "Snowball."

The puppy pawed at the blankets and licked her face.

"Don't tell anyone. I had to smuggle him in."

"If we get caught, do you know any law enforcement officers that might owe you a favor?"

"One or two," he replied.

He grinned, revealing his even, white teeth.

Her eyes misted. "I've missed this little guy."

"He missed you too."

Shane stood and swung the strap of the duffel bag over his head, then set it on the bed. "There's something else."

"This is plenty." She scratched Snowball behind the ears. "I have everything I need."

Shane lifted a cupcake with a single candle on the top. "Happy birthday."

Tears leaked from the corners of her eyes and she sniffled. "How did you know?"

"I cheated. When you applied to rent the town house, I did the background check. Your birthday was listed."

"I can't believe you remembered."

"Well, I can't take too much credit. When you mentioned that no one ever forgot Christmas, something kept bugging me. I didn't figure it out until this morning, or I would have brought you something nicer."

"This is perfect." She touched his sleeve. "You wore that shirt on our first date."

He blushed. "I have others."

"I like this one."

"Then I'm glad I wore it."

"I have a confession."

His expression grew serious. "What's that?"

"When you first asked me out for coffee, I didn't think you were sincere. I heard there was a bet going around town. People wanted to see who could get a date with the new girl first. Seemed like every single man in town brought a healthy dog to the clinic and asked me out."

"I'd never—"

She pressed two fingers against his lips. "I know that now. But that night, I figured I'd just get it over with. I'd let you win and then maybe everyone would move on to something else. I got to the coffee shop first, and when you walked in, you were wearing this shirt. There were creases in the sleeves like you'd just bought it off the shelf at Stetson's Clothing that day."

He chuckled. "I did."

"You'd shaved. You still had a little nick on your chin." She gestured to her face to mark the spot. "That's when I realized it was a real date. That you'd asked me out because you liked me."

"I did. I do. I'm sorry you didn't know that right away."

"You said once that you felt like I was always waiting for you to fail. And I suppose I was. But not in the way you think. It seemed like every time I was happy, truly happy, something went wrong. That's what you were seeing. I was never disappointed in you. Only in myself."

Shane reached over Snowball and clasped her hands. "You don't have to explain. After what happened, you never have to apologize for anything."

"I do though. I need to explain. You were honest with me about your family, and I want to be honest with you.

I didn't tell you the whole story of what happened in Florida."

He shook his head. "I was wrong before. I was wrong to pressure you to share with me. I should have been patient. I should have given you space instead of making demands."

"I've had all the space I need." She touched a bit of stubble he'd missed on his chin when he'd shaved. "Now I want to talk."

He caught her fingers against his cheek. "Then I'm listening."

She stared into his eyes, ready to finally let go of the past. "I used to shoplift. I knew it was wrong, but I didn't care. I was sick of going without all the time. Then, one day, I stole something expensive, a phone, and I got caught. I was looking at jail time. At being a felon. I was about to go to jail when Jack was shot. Then WITSEC offered to relocate me, and I jumped at the chance. The charges against me were dropped."

"You're not that person anymore."

"I know that now. I don't condone the person I was, but I forgive her." She stared into Snowball's liquid brown eyes. Had she ever been that innocent? That trusting? "I should have told you earlier, but I was ashamed."

She lifted her gaze and discovered Shane's face inches from hers.

"Can I kiss you?" he asked.

Her stomach curled. "Yes."

He leaned forward and their lips brushed together. Without taking a breath, he kissed her again, his mouth moving against hers—warm and soft and right. His hand slid to the nape of her neck, and he drew her in closer.

Snowball squirmed between them.

She treasured the feeling of his arms around her. She held him close, relishing the feeling. In that instant, she knew what it felt like to belong.

He pulled away but kept his arms around her.

"I know about shame," he said. "And you're not the only one who can forgive."

All of her uncertainty vanished in an instant. The bridge between them was complete. They still had work to do. Both of them had a lot of bad habits they needed to work on, but as long as they worked together, they had a chance.

Snowball barked. They burst into laughter and separated, allowing the puppy a little breathing space.

"I hope you like dogs," she said. "Eileen came and saw me earlier. Walt's mom left the land to the wildlife trust, just like you thought. He left the dogs to me. He also left me his savings. He ordered me to pay off my student loans." She reached past Shane to the side table. "She also brought me this."

The money was enough to pay off her loans and then some. She didn't want to take it, but Eileen wouldn't listen to her doubts. A bullet had killed Walt, but the cancer invading his body had almost gotten him first. He'd known he was dying. Maybe that's why he'd argued. Maybe that's why he hadn't backed down. She'd never know. She didn't suppose it mattered anymore.

"Were you going to show me something?" Shane asked.

"Oh. Yes. Of course."

She held the large envelope aloft.

Shane lifted an eyebrow. "What's that?"

"It's the deed. Walt sent it to Eileen. He'd put it in his mailbox at the end of the drive. The postman didn't realize it right away. Turned out, we crushed the mailbox during our escape."

Shane gaped. "It was in his mailbox all along?"

"Yep."

"What happens now?"

"Well, Walt's mom left the land to the wildlife trust. Since the hot springs were technically his land, as well, they'll go to the wildlife trust too."

Shane threw back his head and laughed. Snowball perked his ears and stared at him.

"I know I shouldn't be laughing. It's just, well, it's fitting somehow, isn't it?"

"Yes." She gazed at his handsome face and thought about how nice it would be to look at that face every day. "I heard once that love is two people trying to heal each other."

"And here we are."

She straightened and smoothed her atrocious hospital gown. If he could kiss her while she was wearing this, he must really like her.

She crossed her arms. "Even though my cover wasn't compromised beyond you, and I can stay in Kodiak Springs, I think it's time to start over."

He was here. He'd kissed her. He'd been brave the first time around, and now it was her turn.

He tilted his head. "How do we do that?"

She thought back to the first time she'd seen him. She didn't believe in love at first sight, but there'd been something there between them that very first day. He'd risked his life for her. And that wasn't even the best part about him. The best part about him was knowing that was just the kind of person he was. He'd protected her with his whole heart.

"Would you like to meet me for a cup of coffee sometime?"

He glanced at her askance. "As long as this isn't part of some game you're playing with me. You know, see who can take the trooper out for coffee first."

"Nope." She smiled. "No game. I really like you."

"All right then." He leancd in for another kiss. "I'll be there."

SIXTEEN

Exactly one year to the day after Kara asked Shane out on their official starting-over date, she was sitting in a dogsled. The dogs galloped ahead, and Snowball loped beside them. He wasn't a runt anymore. He was an enormous, voraciously hungry dog with a boundless supply of energy. He wasn't old enough to pull a sled yet, but he was getting used to the harness and learning the commands.

Shane stood behind her as musher. They'd spent the past year learning about each other. Shane had taught her about fly fishing and rock climbing and pan-frying fish over an open flame. She'd taught him everything she knew about dogsledding, baking bread and college football.

They still butted heads occasionally, each of them falling back into old habits, but they always managed to work through the setbacks. As the months drifted past, the stumbling blocks grew fewer and farther between, and they each worked on building better, healthier skills.

She still thought about her mom sometimes, but she'd learned to accept that some people couldn't be fixed, and it was better to let them go.

The wind whipped at her cheeks, and the snow stretched out before them, as clean and crisp as a freshly laundered cotton sheet. She glanced over her shoulder and her heart expanded until she felt as though her chest might explode. She'd wondered what it would be like to be loved by Shane. Turned out, it was better than anything she could have imagined.

He wrestled the dogs to a halt, giving them both a chance to savor the gorgeous scenery and the beautiful day.

"You're becoming quite the musher," she said.

He stepped off his perch and stood beside her. "I learned from the best."

She inhaled a lungful of crisp, cold air. "The Walt Tsosie Memorial Wildlife Preserve is really something, isn't it?"

"It sure is."

The resort had sat abandoned on the land until an anonymous donor had offered to transform the building into offices. The Wildlife Foundation had relocated. Most of the people who'd worked at the resort now had jobs there. Even Mark. She'd expected him to leave after what happened, but he proved to be tougher than all of them gave him credit for. He even joined them for dinner on occasion.

Shane rummaged around in the duffel bag at her feet. "Look what I found."

He lifted a single cupcake with a single candle. "Happy birthday."

"I love you."

"I love you too."

"I'll never get tired of hearing you say that."

"I'll never get tired of saying it."

He'd insisted on packing the sled that day, and she

soon understood why. He produced a thick wool blanket and spread it over the snow. Then he set out a tray along with a vase and a single rose. After that he retrieved a thermos of coffee and two mugs.

Kara pressed her hands over her heart. "What else have you got in there?"

He reached for her hand. "Have a seat."

She sat on the blanket, her legs tucked to the side. He sat across from her.

She looked away, and when she looked back, Shane was holding a white-gold ring with a wooden inlay. The look on his face was unbelievably tender and heartbreakingly tentative. Almost unsure.

Her breath hitched. "It's beautiful."

"You told me you didn't like to wear jewelry with raised gemstones at work. When I saw this, I thought you might like this instead."

She smiled, and her eyes filled with tears. "I love it. I love you."

"I was hoping you'd say that." He cleared his throat. "I love what we have together, but I want more. I want a family. I want a family with you. I want a house filled with barking dogs and noisy children and a mudroom full of coats and boots. I want your beautiful butterscotch eyes to be the first thing I see in the morning, and the last thing I see at night. I want to love you when you're happy and I want to comfort you when you're sad. I want to marry you." He tugged on his hat. "Now I need to know if you want that too."

"You have to mean it, you have to really mean it, because I want a big, messy life and I want you by my side. I want to love you until we're old and feeble. So you have to be sure, really sure, this is what you want."

He slid the ring over her finger. "I've never been more sure of anything in my life."

She laughed and her heart felt light, without the weight of shame and guilt weighing her down. She leaned forward and kissed him. "I also want to kiss you. A lot."

"I can get on board with that."

Their lips met again, and her heart thrilled at his caress. He slid his hands behind her back, pulling her even closer. Everything about him felt good and right. They didn't stop kissing until Snowball started barking at them.

They sprang apart with a laugh.

Shane straightened. "Wait a second. You never answered me. Is that a yes?"

Kara moved across the blanket and sat with her back against his chest. "Yes. As many stars as there are in the Alaskan skies, yes."

"You're so beautiful."

She tweaked his beard. "You're not so bad yourself. Is it too soon to ask if we can have a Christmas wedding?"

"Are you afraid I'll forget our anniversary?"

"Never."

"Then absolutely. As long as you mean the Christmas in two days and not the one next year."

She tipped back her head and glanced up at him. "Do you think we can put something together that fast?"

"Where there's a will, there's a way."

She snuggled close and silently thanked God for sending this man to her to love. He was her friend and the love of her life. He was home.

She was home.

* * * * *

If you liked this story from Sherri Shackelford,
check out her previous Love Inspired Suspense books:

No Safe Place
Killer Amnesia
Stolen Secrets

Available now from Love Inspired Suspense!

Find more great reads at
www.LoveInspired.com.

Dear Reader,

Thank you for reading *Arctic Christmas Ambush*! I hope you enjoyed Kara and Shane's story. Alaska's motto is North to the Future. The motto was chosen in 1967 during the Alaska Purchase Centennial and is meant to represent Alaska as a land of promise. What better place to set a story about self-discovery? Shane and Kara are challenged by the land and by each other to imagine a better future together.

I love connecting with readers and would love to hear your thoughts on this story! If you are interested in learning more about this book—or other books and series I have written—I have more information on my website: sherrishackelford.com. I can also be reached by email at sherri@sherrishackelford.com, and snail mail, PO Box 116, Elkhorn, NE 68022.

Happy reading!
Sherri Shackelford